AIR FORCE ONE

AIR FORCE ONE

a novel by
Max Allan Collins

based on the screenplay
written by
Andrew W. Marlowe

BALLANTINE BOOKS • NEW YORK

Motion picture artwork and photography copyright © 1997 Columbia Pictures Industries, Inc. All rights reserved.

All rights reserved under International and Pan-American Copyright Conventions. Published in the United States by Ballantine Books, a division of Random House, Inc., New York, and simultaneously in Canada by Random House of Canada Limited, Toronto.

http://www.randomhouse.com

Library of Congress Catalog Card Number: 97-93637

ISBN 0-345-41975-8

Manufactured in the United States of America

First Edition: August 1997

10 9 8 7 6 5 4 3 2 1

To Elizabeth Beier
who got something out of it after all

"Ask not what your country can do for you,
but what you can do for your country."
—JOHN F. KENNEDY

"The buck stops here."
—HARRY S. TRUMAN

Chapter One_____

The first step was a killer.

The ramp of the MC-130 Hercules turboprop extended into the vast darkness with only the glimmering lights of the city, nineteen thousand feet below, to catch them. The wind in their faces was a howling beast agitated by the mechanical whir of the bulky transport's propellers. These six young men, wearing assault black, were waiting to take that doozy of a step, combat-ready Special Forces staring down into blackness and firefly flickering, faces cold, stomachs churning. Volunteers in a peacetime army, waiting to perform what some would consider an act of mercy for an oppressed people, and others would call a barbarous act of war. Waiting to invade foreign soil . . .

Their jump masters— one on either side of the yawning gateway into nothingness, where the boys in jump packs and combat gear were poised for a leap into possible death and/or glory—bore faces as lined and weathered as those of their charges were smooth and youthful. One of these seasoned veterans wore the uniform of the United States Air Force. The other wore a uniform of his branch of the military—Russian army.

The Russian jump master barked in the tongue his men understood, "Fifteen seconds to release."

And in English, the American jump master, working his voice above the howling wind, told his men, "Stand by . . . stand by . . . *go!*"

And without a moment's hesitation, the six young men—responding to orders in two languages—took that step into darkness.

And history.

Nondescript office buildings clustered about the more distinctive, somber edifice that was the Kazakhstan statehouse, as if guarding it; but that job actually belonged to the solitary sentinel walking the length of the roof of the formidable structure. In his old-style Soviet uniform—which was both a fashion and political statement, courtesy of the charismatic leader around whom many in Kazakhstan had rallied—the guard felt proud, important; but then, it was early in his watch. There would be time for boredom as the night wore on.

Or, on most nights, there would have been.

On this night, the guard—who was young, but not as young as the commandos who were floating down unseen above him, their parachutes as black as the night they were part of—would not live long enough to experience the natural boredom of his duty. He, of course, was unaware of this, just as he was unaware of the red dot of laser light dancing unsteadily on the back of his head, beneath his military cap, just above where his neck began. Like a nervous bug, the red dot skittered and jittered, clinging to him as he patrolled the lonely rooftop.

The commando above—Ron Petersen, Mobile, Alabama—was having difficulty keeping a steady bead on his target; but as hundreds of yards slipped away in fleeting seconds, the rooftop bright as day (seen through the eyes of nightvision goggles), the guard was an ant who gradually became a man, and the red dot steadied.

And the guard—Gregor Ivanovich, Stavropol, Kazakhstan—experienced no pain when his head exploded in a shower of blood, bone, and brain matter. It had been too quick for the pain to register, and there was no sound either, no scream, and the shot had been silenced, no sound at all until his body dropped to the rooftop with his shattered head making a melon-squish punctuation to the whump of the corpse hitting.

That sound was sufficient, however, to alert the rooftop guards on the adjoining buildings, and being alerted caused their own red dots to move from the back of their head to the front, East Indian style, eyes widening as they raised their attention to the silenced shots coming down to silence them.

The six commandos from two countries dropped easily, almost pillow-soft, to the rooftop, the black clouds of their parachutes billowing after them. They were stepping from their gear before their parachutes had even settled, six men in black moving with precision, cloaked in silence, planting small plastic-explosive-laden devices here and there around the rooftop.

Strike Force Leader Joseph Peniston—Brooklyn, New York—motioned the men toward the rooftop access door, which was, of course, exactly where the reconnaissance maps had said it would be, and—much as they had at the mouth of the ramp in the Herc above—they stood poised, positioned, at that doorway, waiting for their leader's signal.

As intelligence reports had informed them, the door—which like the building itself was timeworn—was no problem; the first man in position put his shoulder into it, popped it open to the accompaniment of crunching, near-rotted wood, and soon the six men were charging down a narrow stairway not quite as dark as the night they'd just dropped down through, but close.

Things were about to get even darker. Commando Feydor Ostrov—Moscow, Russia—found the junction box in the hallway, exactly as mapped, threw the lever, and sent the statehouse into pitch-black chaos.

Viewing the world through nightvision goggles, the six-man task force moved into the upper-floor hallway, leaving an American and a Russian on either side of the stairway, assuming point position as the other four commandos rushed on, weapons in hand. Behind them, down the hall, came shouts in Russian as statehouse guards, guns and flashlights in hand, responded to the invasion, moving into the darkness where they were met by bullets from the silenced handguns of the commando point men by the stairway. More shouts followed, and screams, and some return gunfire; but mostly bodies thumping, as guards tumbled dead or dying to the hallway floor.

Simultaneously, other statehouse guards were defending their dominion, bursting through the doorway into the relative spaciousness of their leader's bedroom.

But their leader—General Ivan Stravanovitch Radek—was not calmed by their attention, expressed as it was by flashlights strobing through the darkness, shouts of alarm and confusion, and the disturbing cacophony of armed uniformed men colliding with one another.

General Radek—a high-cheekboned middle-aged man with cold eyes and untamed eyebrows, sitting up in his nightshirt, like a parent woken by rambunctious children— was still thick with sleep when his well-meaning men rushed toward the elaborately carved wooden bed where he rested. Even so, his surprise immediately melded with irritation—could these panicky buffoons be among the crack troops under his command?

Before he could voice a reprimand, however, the guards rushing toward him began to pitch forward, tumbling toward him, onto the floor, even onto the bed, shot dead with the very sort of precision Radek expected from his men, although the men who had delivered those well-aimed silenced shots were not his. They were men in black, goggled men with guns.

Two commandos rushed the general while two more took point position at either side of the bedroom door. Radek began to rise from his bed, to show them just who they were dealing with; before he could so much as speak, a strip of duct tape covered the open wound of his mouth. The general struggled, but the two commandos hauled him out of the bedroom and into the hallway, as easily as if he were a rolled-up carpet.

Outside, an HH-3 helicopter swooped over the sleeping city, churning air, descending to the roof, setting down. Shortly the six men of the two-country commando squad emerged from the now doorless access door, moving quickly across the roof where their two jump masters awaited to provide armed backup. General Radek was on his feet now, or anyway technically speaking he was: two of the team were dragging him along, toward the waiting copter.

The general's crack troops finally arrived—or at least another gaggle of statehouse guards found their way to the roof, to join the fray, opening fire on the departing commandos. Mounted machine guns on the chopper returned fire, raining bullets on the outgunned guards, cutting them down, sending them torn and twisted to the rooftop, their defense meager, their leader, their general, gone.

But one commando—Ron Petersen of Mobile, the man who had first opened fire in this small war—caught a nine-millimeter dose of karma in the back of his neck. Two of his fellow commandos—an American on one arm, a Russian on the other—pulled him into the chopper, and as it lifted into the sky, machine guns spitting lead, Ron Petersen of Mobile drowned in his own blood.

Below, on the rooftop, the toy soldiers took aim at the vacating copter, finally managing some organization, finally mustering some firepower, finally performing in a manner that might have done their general proud, had it stopped his kidnapping, which of course it did not.

Nor, in their zeal to respond to this atrocity, did any of the statehouse guards notice the small flashing red light atop the bundle of plastic explosive at the roof's edge. And as they fired their weapons up toward the copter, smaller and smaller in the sky, blasting bullets upward with no apparent realization that their general was in the line of fire, they experienced, on that cold night, one brief moment of dawn before their existences winked out.

That moment of dawn lasted longer for the living in that departing copter, silhouetted as it was by the blossoming fireball of the exploding roof. The general, shoved into a seat, bound by more bands of duct tape, looked down at this tragedy with eyes wide under the wild eyebrows, his face painted orange by the glow.

Strike Force Leader Peniston glanced at his duct-taped passenger, and spoke into his headset.

"Archangel," he said, "this is Restitution. . . . The package is wrapped."

But not without a price.

The young man from Mobile, soaking in his own blood, the focus of the eyes of the surviving young men in the copter around him, was the first casualty of President James Marshall's war on terrorism.

And not the last.

Chapter Two_____

In a city of golden onion domes rising above ancient churches, a place where picturesque wooden houses lined narrow winding streets, where department stores sought to maintain the tone of an Oriental bazaar and even modern railroad stations attempted to mimic the baroque grandeur of this country's traditions, the President of the United States was having dinner.

And James Marshall—fifty years of age, in the third year of his first term of office, doing well in the popularity polls, "ruggedly handsome" (according to *People* magazine), his sandy-brown hair touched with gray at the temples—was wary of this Moscow banquet.

Warned off Russian cuisine by former President Bush (who should, after all, know something about the dangers of foreign dining), he found himself pleasantly surprised. It had all been quite delicious—the requisite borscht, black caviar on thin pancakes (*blini*), a tiny casserole of sour cream and mushrooms (*zhulienn*), a basil, dill, and green onion salad (*travi,* no lettuce in sight), and a lamb shish kebab (*shashlik*).

Grace and Alice would have enjoyed this feast, but instead he'd suggested they eat at their hotel and take in the Bolshoi, which would get out just in time for their scheduled departure on Air Force One. The First Family and their Secret Service retinue had stayed at the modern Mezhdunarodnaia, the International Hotel, fittingly a joint business venture of Russian and American investors. This banquet was in the Natisonal, a turn-of-the-century hotel in the grand tradition, with a dining room overlooking Red Square.

His Russian counterpart, Stolicha Petrov, had assured Marshall that the absence of the First Lady and their daughter was no breach of protocol, and had graciously allowed Marshall to leave unexpressed his own fears about their presence here this evening.

For all of Petrov's vaunted security (ex-KGB, for Christ's sake) and his own Secret Service contingent, Marshall was apprehensive. Russia was a country torn by past conflicts that simply would not let go of the present. Within Petrov's own ranks—a trusted guard, hell, a damn *waiter* serving caviar—could be a traitor, a spy, even an assassin.

Three former presidents, on three separate occasions, had given Marshall almost identical heart-to-heart talks on the subject of learning to live with (as one of them had rather archly but no less sincerely put it) the "hovering specter of death," the "ever-present companion" (as another described it) of assassination.

And all three had told him that he must reconcile himself to it, get beyond it, but at the same time (and he vividly remembered Gerald Ford's words) "keep your loved ones out of harm's way."

So tonight President Marshall dined in the company of various Russian dignitaries and other of Moscow's elite, not to mention representatives of the international news media. He was, of course, seated at the head table with President Petrov, waiting to deliver an after-dinner speech to the hundreds of men and women seated at round banquet tables before him.

This would not be your ordinary after-dinner speech, however; no parade of homilies about the new fellowship between these great sovereign nations. It would, in fact, be a speech that would shake things up. Not the sort of speech he wanted to give in a Moscow hotel banquet room in the presence of his wife and child, thank you; not the sort of speech that the two men standing at the back of the room, bracketed between Secret Service and Russian plainclothes security, were expecting to hear.

Or, for that matter, would want to hear.

Jack Doherty, national security adviser, and Lloyd Shepherd, White House chief of staff, were, like many of Marshall's team, relatively young men. Doherty, with his short hair, crisp business suit, and blankly efficient persona, had a background that included both Harvard and the United States Army; Shepherd—bespectacled, slightly rumpled, yet still linebacker lean—had been with Marshall forever, that is since the first of Marshall's two terms as governor of Iowa. And like Marshall, Shepherd was a University of Iowa grad; they had met there in the early seventies.

"He's up to something," Shepherd whispered to Doherty.

A frown creased Doherty's perfectly pressed face. "You don't think . . . He wouldn't . . ."

"He's got that look."

"I'll kill him."

Shepherd raised an eyebrow. "You won't be the only one with that sentiment."

Finally, President Petrov, rotund, silver-haired, sixty-five, rose and sidled to the microphone at the podium; behind him, draped against the dark ornate woodwork, were the flags of the United States of America, Russia, and the Commonwealth.

He began to speak, in Russian: "On behalf of the Russian Federation and the Commonwealth of Independent States, I wish to thank you, ladies and gentlemen, for joining us on this historic occasion."

Petrov's voice echoed throughout the high-ceilinged banquet room; but Marshall's ears were treated to an English translation—courtesy of an attractive, dark-haired woman seated next to him.

She whispered, "When the glowing embers of communism sparked a wildfire that threatened to burn away our hard-earned freedom, one world leader was courageous enough to stand at our side, and help us douse the flame."

Petrov continued, as did the young woman's translation: "Tonight we acknowledge the special debt of gratitude we owe that world leader. That man. Ladies and gentlemen . . ."

And the President of Russia lifted his wineglass.

". . . I give you my friend—the President of the United States of America."

The room rang with the clinking of glasses, cheers, and applause as Marshall rose; he was unaware that his mouth was twitching in that familiar, self-deprecating smile that some believed was the most valuable—and cynical—weapon in his public-relations arsenal. But in truth, the smile was as real as it was involuntary.

James Marshall was a rarity among world leaders: his ego had never ballooned into egomania.

And the cheers, the applause, the toasting embarrassed more than pleased him. He was all too aware that a young man, a soldier of the United States Army, under his command, had died; beyond that, other men had died in the raid on the Kazakhstan statehouse—"enemy" soldiers, yes, but flesh-and-blood men with families, lives that had been snuffed out, as a direct result of his orders. Such actions were not worthy of applause; such actions were the stuff sleepless White House nights were made of.

Shaking Petrov's hand, exchanging smiles with the Russian leader, Marshall quieted the acclaim with a gentle hand, settling in behind the podium. The room hushed.

He spoke in Russian; his knowledge of the language was somewhat rudimentary—a year of it in college—and he had worked hard with a coach (taking time that Shep had suggested might be better spent on other matters) to master the opening of his speech.

"President Petrov," Marshall said, "Commonwealth presidents, distinguished guests . . . Please join me in a moment of silence for the victims of the Kazakhstan massacres."

The room was already silent; but all around the hall, heads were bowed, as thoughts and prayers went to those who had suffered, and died, at the hands of the madman Radek, who had forced Marshall's hand with that commando raid.

The memorized Russian portion of his speech over, Marshall withdrew from his pocket his prepared statement, in English, and smoothed it out on the lectern.

Speaking English now, slowly, pausing to allow the young woman to speak her translation into another microphone at a side podium, Marshall continued: "Three weeks ago, American *and* Russian forces, in a cooperative mission of mercy . . ."

In the back of the room, Doherty whispered to Shepherd: "That's stretching it a little, isn't it?"

"One man's mission of mercy," Shepherd said, "is another's act of terrorism."

". . . to apprehend Kazakhstan's self-proclaimed premier, General Ivan Stravanovitch Radek. This vicious dictator's campaign of terror has given new meaning, and an added resonance, to the word *atrocity*."

Around the hall, as the translated words were assimilated, faces were tight with shared outrage, heads nodding.

"From the moment he seized power," Marshall continued, "Radek sought to break the will of democracy and restore an empire of tyranny. But as a result of the cooperative effort of our two countries, of our act of collective security, this threat to the world community now awaits trial for crimes against humanity."

The audience began to applaud—not wildly; respectfully. Marshall turned the page of his speech, considered the rest of the words that Shepherd and others had prepared for him—and folded the sheets of paper and returned them to his side suit pocket.

"What the hell's he doing?" Doherty asked.

Shepherd sighed, removed his glasses.

"Tell me he's not going to . . ."

Shepherd cleaned his glasses on his tie.

Doherty said, "Shit. How many times have I told him . . ."

"Presidents don't make extemporaneous speeches," Shepherd said, in a zombie monotone. "You don't make policy off the cuff."

"God help us."

"Fasten your seat belt," Shepherd said.

"Stay a politician long enough," Marshall was saying, "and you hear yourself uttering phrases like *collective security,* and *world community.*"

Marshall laughed gently, with that half smile that immediately had his audience smiling with him, even before they heard the translation. And he continued, speaking in the easy, conversational manner that had won him the presidency (his shy self-deprecation in those town-hall meetings had made mincemeat of the too slick incumbent).

"You give meaningless speeches and act awfully proud of yourself, of your . . . *golden* words." The smile was gone. "But what do golden words mean to a ten-year-old girl, raped before her parents' eyes? Parents who were then murdered before *her* eyes? Or to the crying infants who were used for bayonet practice? While we discussed the 'Radek problem' within the confines of polite civilization, in our halls of dignified discourse, whole villages were gunned down. Burned down. Human beings . . . roasted alive."

A funereal silence had settled upon the hall, at the back of which a dismayed Doherty glanced at Shepherd, who shrugged and said, "It'll be fun to see what they pull as a sound bite, don't you think?"

"For three weeks," Marshall said, "I've been haunted by doubt."

"Thanks for sharing," Doherty said glumly.

"Make no mistake," Marshall continued, "I do not doubt our action. I find no fault with the brave men of our two countries who surgically removed a cancer from Kazakhstan."

"I don't know," Shepherd said. "Maybe we oughta start letting him contribute a few thoughts to his speeches, in the future. He turns a nice phrase."

"I wish he'd just stick to the goddamn script," Doherty breathed.

"But for two hundred thousand victims," Marshall said, jaw firm, eyes tight with anger, "we acted too slowly. While we attempted to negotiate a political solution, thousands upon thousands died, unnecessarily. And I say to the Russian people, search your conscience, as I am searching the American conscience."

"I really don't like the sound of this," Doherty said.

"Ask yourself the question I would ask the American people, and their elected representatives—would we have acted against this . . . this monster if, after torturing his own people, he had not decided to threaten our own peace and security?"

Marshall's eyes searched the room, as if seeking the answer to the question he'd posed, even as hundreds of eyes gazed back him, waiting for him to answer it himself.

He did: "For the sake of history, for the sake of humanity, and for the sake of all of our children, the answer must be *yes* . . . yes, we would have acted!"

"Great," Doherty said. "He just appointed himself police chief of the world."

"Quiet," Shepherd said.

"Let us assure the world tonight that from this day

forward, we will no longer turn away from our responsibility to humankind. And to those of you who use terror to strike fear into our hearts, to those of you who confuse politics with atrocity, hear these words: Your day has ended."

"Sound bite," Doherty said glumly.

"We will no longer tolerate, we will no longer negotiate and we will no longer live in fear. . . ." Marshall looked out into the crowd with a gunfighter squint. "It's the terrorist's turn to live in fear."

"There's your sound bite," Shepherd said.

"Yeah," Doherty said woefully. "I think you're probably right—the President of the U.S. challenging terrorists to 'make his day'—that might make the evening news at that."

Marshall stepped away from the lectern. The audience was cloaked in silence, a stunned silence, the silence of a group of people who understood they were in the presence of, and a small part of, history.

And, finally, one of those footnotes in history began to clap. Others joined in. And as President Petrov again shook Marshall's hand, the ovation became a standing one, building to a crescendo that echoed through the room like machine-gun fire, the first volley in a new war.

This applause Marshall accepted without the shy smile.

This applause he received gratefully, this applause he took into himself like nourishment, feeding not his ego, but his resolve.

*Chapter Three*_____

Fifty minutes from midtown Moscow, constructed in an age when air travel was for the privileged, Shere metievo Airport—serving thirty-four major international airlines—was clogged with Jewish immigrants, Armenian refugees, Vietnamese smugglers, American and European tourists, Russian mafia mules, and black marketeers of various nations. Its sprawling terminals spread out to runways like tentacles of a sluggish beast whose parasites scurried beneath it, subjects of its bored, benign neglect. Travel here was a slow process, all bottleneck and no flow—except, of course, for the privileged. Communism might come and go, but some things never changed.

Bathed in floodlights, perched majestically on a runway, dwarfing nearby commuter and military jets, stood a Boeing 747-200 with the bold inscription THE UNITED STATES OF AMERICA above a royal-blue stripe over a thin gold line that tapered to a tail adorned with the American flag and the presidential seal.

The presence of Air Force One on this moderately cold evening prompted extra security measures at a facility already top-heavy with armed guards. Russian soldiers patrolled outer checkpoints while U.S. Air Force security guards watched the aircraft's perimeter. Secret Service agents guarded all entrances, inside and out of the adjacent terminal, while reporters and White House aides passed through an inspection barrier, also manned by the Secret Service.

Melanie Mitchell, deputy press secretary, had already been admitted through the Secret Service checkpoint. A striking dark-haired woman of thirty-three, she stood in the shadow of a wing, chatting with several AFO crew members, waiting for the arrival of some very special guests. The evening chill made her breath visible, but Melanie had already deposited her coat aboard the ship; looking crisply businesslike in her navy-blue suit, Melanie should have been exhausted. This had been another brutally long day. But she was relishing every moment of this, her first trip to Moscow, and savoring the responsibility she'd been entrusted with, as liaison to the first Russian news team ever allowed aboard AFO.

Like an apparition, the Russian news van emerged from the darkness of the runway, moving quickly enough to startle and alert the normally unflappable Secret Service agents at the barrier. After a screeching stop, the six-man news team, casual in leather jackets, sweaters, and jeans, carry-ons and equipment bags in hands and slung over shoulders, climbed out of the van.

Veteran Agent Gibbs—blond, blandly handsome— stepped forward with clipboard in hand.

"Gentlemen," he said, "welcome to Air Force One. Please present your gear to Special Agent Walters for inspection."

The pale, dark-haired man who stepped forward from

the little group had a ready smile and piercing eyes in a spade-bearded, boyish countenance. He wore a dark green ribbed sweater and his leather jacket was a dark brown that seemed nearly black.

"Ivan Korshunov," he said, extending his hand to Gibbs. "Segment producer, *600 Seconds*."

The special agent's expression was noncommittal as he said, "Gibbs," and gave the Russian producer's hand a quick shake. "Now, if you'll show your equipment to Special Agent Walters . . ."

"Is that necessary?" Korshunov made a casual head gesture back toward his van. "We were just inspected at the gate."

"Sir," Gibbs said with just a hint of acid in his smooth voice, "this plane carries the President of the United States. Although we wish to express your press service every courtesy, you'll have to follow our security measures to the letter. Is there a problem?"

"No," Korshunov said. "Of course not. I'm terribly sorry."

Melanie, overhearing all this, had to hold herself back from interceding; as much as she wanted to pave the way for the Russian news team, she knew enough not to challenge the Secret Service.

With runway roar in her ears, she stood quietly, on her side of the barrier, while Gibbs checked Korshunov and his news crew through, using the ID pad of a portable computer to ID their thumbprints; in each instance, the computer matched the thumbprint with a dossier and photograph, and, six times, the word CLEARED flashed upon the liquid-crystal screen.

It took a while for Special Agent Walters, with the help

of several air-force security guards and bomb-sniffing German shepherds, to go through the video cameras, sound equipment, and other supplies, from carry-ons and shoulder bags to the fiberglass-foam-padded flight cases that ensconced the heavier gear. Some of the equipment required dismantling, but the news crew—and Korshunov—voiced no further complaints. The dogs made more noise than they did.

Melanie was relieved Korshunov had backed down. *600 Seconds* was an enormously popular show in Russia, with a Western-style, fast-paced, quick-cutting, irreverent approach; but its stance was reactionary. There had been much discussion about whether or not to allow the *600 Seconds* team aboard Air Force One.

Ultimately, it was the President who said, literally, "Hell, yes."

And if anyone could win them over, it would be James Marshall. In light of the Kazakhstan incursion, positive publicity on a Russian TV show that normally had an anti-American bias would be a real coup. It was risky, but this could be a rare opportunity to win over Russian TV viewers who might normally view that madman General Radek with some degree of sympathy.

"Equipment checks out," the tanned, dark-haired Walters told Gibbs, as the Russians were handed over their gear and bags.

Responding to the permission granted by Gibbs's nod, Melanie said to the AFO crewmen, "Excuse me, fellas—show time!", and moved quickly to greet Korshunov and his team as they moved past the Secret Service barrier.

"*Dobry vechir,* gentlemen," Melanie said, offering her

hand to the approaching Korshunov, working her voice above the runway noise. "Melanie Mitchell, deputy press secretary. I'll accompany you from here."

"Ah, Ms. Mitchell," Korshunov said, clasping her hand warmly. "What a pleasure to finally meet you, in person."

That smile was something; she would have to watch this guy—he had charm to spare.

"The President and I were delighted we could accommodate your request," she said. "I'm sorry about the rites of passage. . . . I'm sure you understand."

"Oh yes," Korshunov said, falling in step as Melanie guided him toward the plane. "Inconvenience is a Moscow tradition."

As they ascended the boarding ramp at the rear of the plane, Melanie glanced back to say, "I understand your program is top-rated for your time slot."

Korshunov worked to be heard over the latest takeoff of an Acroflot Il-86. "We don't have much competition."

She arched an eyebrow. "Hope you won't be too tough on us."

"No more than your *60 Minutes*."

"Ouch." She flashed him half a smile. "That's not necessarily much reassurance."

He flashed a whole one back. "You have nothing to fear from me, Ms. Mitchell."

As they entered the rear cabin, where the press was corralled, Melanie said, "So here's how it works . . . during the flight, two members of your crew will be allowed out of the press area for taping."

This portion of the plane, with its coach-style seating,

was much like any other airliner, though it enjoyed the same, soothing blue-gray color scheme as the rest of AFO. The news team began stowing their carry-ons in the overhead compartments while, in the aisle, Melanie and Korshunov chatted about the ground rules of the air.

Korshunov asked, "How long will we be allowed access to the President?"

"Ten minutes."

"That's not much time, Ms. Mitchell."

"No. But there's a reason this plane is called the Flying White House. The President has business as usual to conduct, and in addition he spends some private time with his family."

Korshunov brightened. "Will we be able to shoot the First Lady and young Alice?"

"Possibly. I can definitely give you access to some of the President's aides, and you may wish to interview the crew members of Air Force One. They all have interesting, human stories to tell."

"I'm sure. But we're here to see the President."

She tried her patented, chin-crinkle smile out on him. "And see him you will. Patience, Mr. Korshunov."

His smile, this time, was almost a kiss. "That's another Moscow tradition, Ms. Mitchell."

"Well, hospitality is an American tradition, Mr. Korshunov," Melanie said cheerily, "and if you'd like, I think we have time for a quick tour."

"I like this American tradition." The somewhat cruel planes of Korshonuv's face were softened by his amiable manner. *This guy should be on-air talent*, Melanie thought. *He's wasted behind the scenes.*

"Then follow me," she said.

"Krasin," Korshunov said, nodding to one of his team, "Bazylev," nodding to another, and two harshly handsome young men followed their leader as he tagged after Melanie. The other three newsmen settled into their coach-style seats; rather burly, they didn't look any too comfortable.

Secret Service agents were positioned here and there along the path as she led Korshunov from the traditional cabin that was the press area into the spacious forward area of the plane. Melanie led the way down the wide hallway at the left of the plane (as you faced forward); occasional Secret Service guards stood watch, and now and then along the curve of the many-windowed wall, presidential staffers were seated, either relaxing or working, in chairs or couches, in the glow of brass lamps affixed to walnut end tables that seemed more apropos to a classy hotel room than an airplane.

At right were the gray-blue fabric-covered walls of the row of cabins that served as offices and staterooms; midway, the row of walls and doors stopped, and dipped into a lounge area with four first-class-style seats facing each other over coffee tables; various staffers were already seated, some working, others reading Tom Clancy under the watchful eye of the presidential seal on a curved wall near an emergency exit. The seal was everywhere on the ship, including the blue aprons of the stewards.

Melanie cracked open a cabin door and revealed a bustling if necessarily cramped office area, where even now aides were busy using phones, faxes, and computers.

"This is our in-flight office," Melanie said redundantly,

then shut the door and gestured to another as they moved on. "Many of the cabins serve a dual purpose—believe it or not, our backup office here could be converted into an operating room."

"Should anyone need open heart surgery," Korshunov said.

"It could happen," Melanie said, chipper. "The presidential physician *is* aboard."

He sighed and his expression seemed admiring. "You've thought of every contingency, haven't you?"

"We have to, Mr. Korshunov."

"You're not showing us into every cabin, Ms. Mitchell. Don't you believe in freedom of the press?"

She waggled a scolding finger back at him, cutely. "Not where certain classified features of this aircraft are concerned, Mr. Korshunov. I can tell you that it's bulletproof, windows and all, and can withstand a nuclear blast . . . depending on our proximity to the epicenter, of course."

"Of course. How comforting."

"There are various areas, on this ship, blocked by Secret Service agents—don't ever try to get past them without an escort. We don't want an international incident, now do we?"

"Certainly not." Korshunov glanced behind him to exchange smiles and nods with Krasin and Bazylev. "We appreciate the warning."

Melanie paused at the curve of a short winding flight of stairs at the bottom of which one of the ever-present Secret Service agents stood watch.

"Mission Communications Center," she said with a

nod toward the door at the top of the winding stairs. "Off-limits, I'm afraid."

"Pretty sophisticated?"

"I would say—possibly the most advanced mobile communications center on the earth . . . or anyway, above it."

Korshunov smiled, sighed. "It is the Flying White House, after all."

"Yes it is," she said. "We could run the entire country from here. . . . We could wage a war."

Korshunov eyed the blue-gray walls. "Peaceful surroundings for a war."

"We're capable of more pleasant communications, as well. Just last week, the President called our shuttle astronauts right from—"

"Melanie!"

It was Gibbs, coming up the hallway quickly.

"The President's about to arrive," the Secret Service agent said. "Get your guests to their seats, would you?"

"Certainly." She smiled at Korshunov. "You know the way back?"

"I believe we can navigate it," Korshunov said affably.

She touched his arm. "Get comfortable, and I'll check back with you in a few minutes. I'll get you a VIP press kit."

Korshunov gave her a nod that was almost a bow, and his men parted deferentially for him to assume the lead position as they headed back to the press cabin.

Melanie had a good feeling about this. There was a definite chemistry between her and the Russian producer; he'd been playful with her about the restrictions she'd presented him, almost as if he were keeping his forceful personality in check. He was attracted to her, she could tell.

This just might be an interesting flight.

*Chapter Four*_____

Red Square retained its name, despite perestroika, as the appellation referred not to communism, but to its grandcur (an alternate meaning of the Russian word for "red" being "beauty"). At night, the austere red walls of the Kremlin, the distinctive spires of St. Basil's, the stately stucco buildings on the east side, the low-slung marble mausoleum of Lenin took on an otherworldly beauty. To James Marshall, it was like gliding through history.

Which, in the back of the presidential limousine, was precisely what he was doing. As the presidential motorcade emerged with its Russian police escort, other Moscow police held back the crowds on the cobblestone all around, as many cheered, and waved tiny American flags. This was a sight in Red Square no other American president had ever witnessed.

Here and there, in the crowd, however, were the more familiar Russian sentiments of anti-Americanism, the reactionary support General Radek enjoyed from a vocal minority of the people—fists were raised in shaking rage, and shouted curses Marshall could not understand (and yet understood perfectly) rang out among the cheers.

Doherty had already scolded him, as they moved through the hotel's promenade to the accompaniment of flash-bulbs popping, photojournalists of a dozen countries lining the corridor. On his one side had been Doherty, on the other Shepherd, with Secret Service fore and aft; the entourage had moved quickly down the great hall.

"Sir," Doherty said, "you really should have let us know what you were planning to say."

"You would have tried to talk me out of it."

"You're damn right I would have tried," Doherty said. "And I would have kept at it till I succeeded!"

Marshall had given him a mild, mildly smug smile. "Now you know why I didn't tell you."

Now, as the motorcade moved down an empty cobble-stone street, the conflicted crowd left behind, Marshall sat in back of the limo with his two most trusted advisers facing him.

"Yeah, thanks, Gary," Shepherd was saying into his Inmar-Sat portable phone, "I'll tell him."

Shepherd flipped the phone shut and slipped it into its slim, satellite-unit briefcase. "We got problems on the farm bill."

Marshall shrugged. "We saw that coming. Any other good news?"

"FEMA wants you to come down and look at the hurricane damage."

Marshall shook his head, grimacing. "Those poor bastards . . . Don't we do enough damage to each other, without God and nature pitching in? Schedule that as soon as possible."

"You got it."

The thrum of wheels rolling over cobblestones provided a quaint backdrop to the pregnant pause that followed.

Then Marshall asked, "Any reaction?"

Shepherd played dumb; it wasn't very convincing. "To what?"

"To the Notre Dame game. To my speech, Shep. It got picked up by satellite; they heard it back home. You remember the speech, Shep—the one that has both of your assholes clenched?"

Doherty, whose countenance had been pallid and pathetic since they got into the limo, tossed a tired smirk at Shepherd.

Shepherd said, "The networks are going to lead with it. . . . Some nice comments on the Russian you spoke."

"If I'd paid more attention in my freshman Russian class," Marshall said, "I wouldn't've had to work so hard at it."

"The problem is, sir—"

"It's just the three of us, Shep. Stick with 'Jim.' It makes me nervous when you call me sir behind closed doors. It makes me think you're unhappy with me."

"All right, Jim," Shep said. "But the problem is, now that it's out there, this 'live in fear' speech as they're already calling it, it's . . . it's going to be very damn hard to back away from."

"Who wants to back away from it?"

Doherty offered a sick smile and gestured with a weak hand. "Every world leader gets caught up in his own hyperbole from time to time, sir . . . Jim—"

"To hell with that," Marshall said. "We're making that speech our new policy. Understood?"

Doherty swallowed, glanced at Shepherd, who shrugged.

Doherty tried the smile again; it was sicker yet. "Perhaps we should schedule a policy review . . . run some numbers . . . seek some input. . . ."

Marshall sat forward. "Look, don't think you can sucker me by sucking up. I know you hate this idea."

Doherty sighed, shook his head. "It's not going to help your numbers."

"Fuck my numbers," Marshall said. "It's the right thing to do, and it's what we're going to do."

"Sir," Shepherd said.

Marshall glared at his friend.

Shepherd said, "Jim . . . if you backed off now, you could resume this opinion *after* the next election."

"I'm going to take that as a vote of approval, this assumption of yours that I'm going to win. But on the off chance I *don't* get reelected, maybe I better do the things I think are worth doing while I still have this job."

Shepherd's frown conveyed as much sympathy as displeasure. "Well, with all due respect . . . sir . . . I don't think inviting terrorists to come to America to dine is gonna help you keep that job."

Marshall snorted a laugh. "I'm sure the loyal opposition's going to make me out a warmonger."

Doherty said to Shepherd, "Show him."

"All right."

The little TV was perched on the floor at an angle all could see, but was mostly for Marshall's benefit. Shepherd used a remote control to hit play on the VCR.

"Here's the kind of support you can expect from the loyal opposition," Shepherd said.

"This was last night," Doherty explained.

On the screen, Larry King, suspenders and all, was

hunched over his desk, saying to his guest, ". . . and your reaction to the President's trip to Moscow—good or bad?"

The corpulent speaker of the house, Franklin Danforth, reminding Marshall of politicians as drawn by Al Capp in "Li'l Abner" (the favorite comic strip of his youth), was intoning pompously in his cornpone drawl, "Criminal, Larry, why it's simply criminal."

"Strong charges."

"Larry, one of our boys died during Marshall's exercise in self-aggrandizement. And for what? So we could proclaim victory over another country's problems? What about our own problems, our own suffering poor, our put-upon middle class?"

Marshall said, "Turn that shit off."

"Just a little more, sir," Shepherd said.

". . . and now he's got the nerve," Danforth was saying, working up as much righteous indignation as a windbag hypocrite could manage, "to prance around Moscow gloating about this 'joint operation,' while that poor young American's family is back home, burying their boy. . . . If I were James Marshall, I'd be ashamed of myself."

"I said, shut it off," Marshall said.

Shepherd did.

"Goddamn him. Making politics of this." Marshall looked out the window into the darkness of the Moscow night. "What does he know about it? I'm the one who had to call the family."

He whipped away from the window and startled his two aides, unaware of the power, the presidential charisma of his glare. "That fat bastard didn't even use that soldier's name. He wasn't a 'boy'—he was Sergeant Ronald

Petersen, and he died in the service of his country, a hero. And I'm proud of him. And so are his parents."

"I wish you'd given *that* speech instead," Doherty said glumly.

They rode in silence until the motorcade arrived at Sheremetievo Airport, when Shepherd reminded Marshall that a news crew from *600 Seconds* would be along on the flight home.

"After that antiterrorist speech," Shepherd said, "they're gonna be on you like cocaine on Marion Barry."

Shepherd had been against allowing the newsmen aboard. Doherty, too.

Doherty said, "Watch your ass . . . sir. Those sons-of-bitches have never made any bones about their support of the old right-wing regime."

"They're fascists," Shepherd said.

"You'd rather I preach to the choir?" Marshall asked. "Then we'd never make any progress."

Soon the presidential limo pulled up in front of Air Force One, haloed in spotlights, an American oasis in this foreign land. The motorcade followed behind, and various dignitaries who had tagged along exited their vehicles to wish the President *dos vidania*. Shaking hands with them, Marshall paid his respects, bid his good-byes, and went up the red-carpeted stairs of the boarding ramp at the front of the plane, where he paused at the top for a final wave, before disappearing into his home, his office, of the sky.

Stepping inside the plane, the President was met by Air Force One's pilot, Air Force Colonel Gregory Axelrod, a reassuringly square-jawed individual with just the right amount of gray at the temples.

"Welcome aboard, Mr. President," Axelrod said, snapping a salute.

Marshall returned the salute, somewhat casually, saying, "Hey, Greg. How do the skies look tonight?"

"Glassy, sir. Clear all the way home."

He formed half a smile. "Maybe I'll finally get a little sleep . . . if I can remember how. . . . Grace and Alice aboard yet?"

"No, Mr. President."

"The ballet run long?"

Axelrod smiled; it was a toothy smile as reassuring as the square jaw. "Exactly. Their ETA is seventeen minutes."

Roger Morgan, one of Marshall's aides, was approaching; he thrust the new briefing papers toward Marshall, who slipped off his jacket, loosened his tie, and accepted them.

"Sir," Morgan said, "the Iraqis have just mobilized two brigades toward the northern border."

"That figures," Marshall said disgustedly. "Moment we ease the damn sanctions . . . Hey, did anybody get the Notre Dame game on tape?"

"It's waiting for you." Morgan grinned. "The fourth quarter was really something—"

Marshall held up a hand. "Stop. The Iraqis, you can fill me in on. Where the game's concerned, don't brief me."

"Sir?"

"Let me be surprised for once."

Morgan nodded, smiled a little, and the President moved to the door of his stateroom; Lieutenant Colonel Dewayne Perkins had gotten to his feet, but Marshall waved him back to the comfortable seat by the brass reading lamp, across from the stateroom door. With the President's permission, the brawny marine settled back down, to get back to his Robert Ludlum, using his attaché case as a desk—this particular attaché case happened to contain doomsday nuclear codes and was known as the nuclear football.

Marshall was halfway through his stateroom door when a familiar voice halted him.

"Mr. President," Shepherd said. "Can we talk?"

"Shep," Marshall said, "give me thirty seconds, would you?"

Shepherd nodded, and Marshall went into the presidential stateroom, well-appointed but no more lavish, really, than a room at a Radisson or Marriott. The President of the United States tossed his suit coat on a chair and collapsed into a weary heap on the couch; he rubbed his eyes, breathing heavily, as if in a deep sleep. Eyes closed, he took a few moments of peace at the end of this breakneck day, which, like all his days, was never really over, and when it was, would merely blend into the next, and the next. Why did he love this job?

A knock at the door. Shep. Marshall had asked for thirty seconds, and his chief of staff had granted him a full sixty. Such generosity should not go unrewarded.

"Yes," Marshall said.

Shepherd entered and closed the door. Marshall swung himself into a sitting position.

"Jim, the Speaker's remarks. They were really over the edge. I believe we're completely justified in issuing a press release objecting to the intemperance of Danforth's language."

Marshall stood and said, "Forget it, Shep," and moved

through the adjoining bathroom into a mini-version of the Oval Office, where he headed to the desk and picked up one of the many phones.

"Steward, please," he said, hung up, and turned to Shepherd, who had followed him. "Shep, a young man gave his life for his country. That bloated asshole Danforth can do and say what he wants. But I'm not going to cheapen Sergeant Petersen's memory, or his sacrifice, by turning him into a goddamn sound bite . . . clear?"

"Clear," Shepherd said, wincing. He dropped a hand to his belly. "Christ, Jim, but you give me ulcers."

"One of the perks of your job."

A knock at the door announced the steward Marshall had summoned.

"Hey, Joey," Marshall said to the young man poised in the doorway, "could you get me a cold one?"

"Anything special, sir?"

"A Heineken. Iciest sucker you can find."

"Yes, sir!"

"No, wait," Shepherd said. "Bring him one of those Russian beers."

The steward paused for a moment, to see if the President would veto that legislation, then when he didn't, disappeared.

"Come on, Shep," Marshall growled. "I've been on a borscht-and-vodka regimen since I got to Moscow. Isn't that enough?"

Shepherd shook his head no. "We've got that Russian *600 Seconds* crew aboard, remember? It'll look good on Rooskie TV."

Marshall, shaking his head, slipped behind his desk,

picked up a stack of policy reports, and began thumbing through. "When in Rome, I suppose."

"More like, *ich bin ein Berliner,* sir."

"If I'm a Berliner, make it a damn Heineken!"

The steward was back shortly with the Russian beer on a small tray. Marshall took it, braved a swig, swallowed hard.

"Not bad," he said. "For piss . . . Joey, pour this swill out and fill the bottle with goddamn Heineken."

The steward grinned. "Yes, Mr. President."

Then the steward was gone, and Marshall was saying, "I don't believe you, Shep. You've reduced me to playing politics with a fucking bottle of beer. . . . Maybe I've been in this office too long."

"Look at the bright side." Shepherd smirked, his arms folded. "After your speech hits the approval ratings, you may not have that problem next year."

Marshall picked up another phone and touched the extension of the AFO's Mission Communication Center.

Within that center, to which earlier Melanie Mitchell had forbidden the Russian news team entry, three airforce specialists manned an elaborate communications post that occupied much of the upper deck, wall-to-wall, top-of-the-line, state-of-the-art computers, video decks, and satellite receivers.

And right now their president was on the horn.

In his office below, Marshall said, "Put on the tape of the Notre Dame game, boys."

And in the high-tech communications center above, an air-force specialist slid a VHS tape into a VCR, using his finely honed mastery of technology to channel the feed to the President's office.

Marshall leaned back in his comfortable swivel chair as a monitor across the room came alive with a football game that had been played across the ocean, that afternoon.

"Shep," Marshall said, "gather Defense and State Department in the conference room in fifteen minutes."

"Sir?"

"We need to review this new Iraq data."

"Yes, Mr. President."

Shepherd slipped out, and Marshall continued shuffling through, quickly scanning the various documents that had been waiting for his attention, stealing occasional moments for glimpses at the big game.

*Chapter Five*_____

Though the President was already aboard Air Force One, a throng of international press—photographers and videographers among them—continued to wait in the no-man's-land between the gate and the Secret Service barrier. A night flight for AFO—particularly on foreign soil—always had the excitement and feel of an opening night or a Hollywood premiere, with the Boeing 747-200 glowing in the darkness, swathed in spotlights as if it were a theater or movie palace, with the arriving President and dignitaries the stars who would wave to an adoring public before disappearing within. All that remained on this opening night was for the President's costars to arrive.

And when the second, smaller motorcade—a single limousine with its fore-and-aft police escort—pulled up near the plane, air-force security guards snapped to attention, a Secret Service agent reduced to livery status opened the rear door, and Grace Marshall stepped lightly from the limo. Her beaming smile competing in illumination with the floodlights that bathed AFO, waving to the crowd as flashbulbs popped, the First Lady was as much a star as anything Broadway or Hollywood had to offer.

Self-assured, not quite aristocratic, Grace Marshall, forty-eight, was as beautiful a First Lady as the White House had seen since Jacqueline Kennedy. Her dark hair in its distinctive shoulder-brushing style (much imitated, as had been Jackie's 'do) framed features dominated by eyes that flashed with intelligence and humor. Peeking out from the blue satin cape, her simple, elegant blue velvet dress looked immaculate, despite the long ballet she'd just sat through; the light caught the sprinkle of diamonds at her throat and winked at the media.

Grace waited, trying not to let her smile look as strained as it felt; her daughter, Alice, was taking her time in the backseat, gathering programs, an autographed pair of ballerina slippers, and other souvenirs of the evening. Alice, of course, had had plenty of time to do that before now. But she was, after all, a teenager, and the chief duty in the life of teenagers is to inconvenience the adults around them.

"Hurry, dear," Grace said, through her smiling teeth, though there was no smile in her voice.

The thirteen-year-old was in no rush, despite being the cause of their twenty-minute-plus delay. Grace was happy her daughter had enjoyed the ballet—Alice was studying dance with a private tutor—but irritated that her headstrong only child had, out of earshot of her mother, coerced their Intourist liaison and a Secret Service agent into taking her backstage to get autographs.

And, of course, once that expedition had been put in motion, it would have been an embarrassment—an international one, at that—to attempt to derail it. So Grace Marshall had gone backstage with her daughter and met those wonderful dancers and their director, every smile, every handshake, every warm expression of admiration (requiring translation by the Intourist guide) further delaying the departure of Air Force One.

"Dear," Grace said, waving at the cameras, caught on the tarmac like some ground-crew member waving in a plane, "your father will have a fit. . . ."

Alice, her oval face and perfect features mirroring her mother's, wearing just the right light touch of makeup for her age, was still lackadaisically gathering her things; her expression, and voice, was sullen as she said, "And *he's* never kept *us* waiting."

"He's the President, dear."

"Really?" Alice said, finally emerging with her armful of Bolshoi memorabilia. "I thought every kid had Secret Service agents outside their bathroom."

And once out into the cool evening air, in both the shadow and the glow of AFO, flashbulbs popping, video cams rolling, Alice's sullen expression was transformed into one of guileless goodness. Waving, beaming, a vision in her short gold lace dress under a black wool coat with fake-fur collar, she was everything the First Daughter should be—shy, sweet, sincere.

Of course, once they were up the ramp and inside Air Force One, she dropped the mask and became the real (and sometimes bratty) child Grace knew all too well. As her daughter moved ahead of her down the hallway, with the cabin doors to their left, Grace followed her toward their stateroom, but the girl halted. They could see a Secret Service agent positioned at the door, alerting them that the President was within.

"Terrific," Alice said. "He's using the stateroom." The child gestured to her gold dress. "I want to get out of this and into something comfortable!"

Slipping her hand onto her daughter's shoulder, Grace said, gently, not looking for a fight, "And if he hadn't been in the stateroom, you'd have been irritated about that. How can a parent win with you?"

"You can't."

She squeezed her daughter's shoulder. "Say hi to your father, tell him about tonight, about the ballet. . . ."

"He's too busy."

"Even if he's in a meeting, you can still stick your head in and say hello."

"No thanks."

"You're in rare form tonight, Alice, even for you."

The child moved ahead, past the Secret Service agent posted at their stateroom door—not inquiring about her father—and flopped into one of the leather first-class-style chairs in the little lounge area between cabins. She tossed her Bolshoi keepsakes on the coffee table before her.

A steward was moving by, and Alice said, "Hey, Joey—could you bring me some cocoa? Cold out there."

"Sure thing," Joey said. "Double whip cream?"

"The works."

Joey scurried off, and Alice said to her hovering mother, "I'm gonna drown my sorrows in fat grams."

"Alice . . ."

The girl's eyes were on the Secret Service agent who stood in front of their stateroom door.

Grace sat next to her slouching daughter. "Do you want me to see if he's in a meeting?"

"He will be. And then when the plane starts to taxi, he'll come out for a second and see us and say, 'Oh, are you guys back? How was the ballet?' But he won't even hear the answer, he'll be on his way to some *other* meeting. Like always."

For a moment Grace could find nothing to say; her daughter was speaking the truth.

"All anybody talks about is the next election," Alice said poutily. "Well, I hope he loses."

The words were like a slap to Grace. "Don't ever say that. This job means everything to your father."

"Oh, you're wrong," the girl said, dripping sarcasm. "His family means everything to him. I read it in his *Rolling Stone* interview."

"He doesn't want it to be like this," Grace said. "You know the kind of responsibilities your father has. He can't put us first, you and I, like I know he wants to."

"He's always been like this."

The girl's father's life had been one of public service for as far back as she could remember.

"But at least," Alice said, "when he was just a governor, he could find time for us on the weekends, sometimes. We could have a real vacation once in a while."

"You just spent four days in Moscow!"

"That's not a vacation. That's . . . diplomacy."

Alice turned away from her mother, looking out the window into the night and the twinkling lights of Sheremetievo.

"Some girls might consider themselves lucky, being the President's daughter," Grace said, her voice trembling with hurt and a little anger. "They might think they were having the experience of a lifetime. It seems to me you were the only American teenage girl at the Bolshoi tonight—and I wonder how many have ever been back-stage? That's something your father gave you . . . that access, that importance. He makes your life special. And you resent him for it."

Alice's sullen expression fell away and she looked at her mother, saw the pain in her mother's eyes, and said, "I'm sorry, Mom . . . the ballet was great. I'll never forget it. Thanks for taking me."

An awkward moment turned into a hug accompanied by laughter.

And the girl bounced up and went up the hallway to the Secret Service agent, asked a question, nodded, then came back, a chipper expression covering her disappointment fairly well.

"Dad's in a meeting," Alice said casually.

Alice and Grace were sitting in the lounge area when Deputy Press Secretary Melanie Mitchell strolled up.

"How's the First Lady and First Daughter, on this chilly Russian evening?"

"Okay," Alice said noncommittally.

"Fine," Grace said. She found the young woman pleasant but a little pushy.

"You know, we have some special guests aboard tonight," Melanie told them.

"Oh yes," Grace said. "That news crew."

"Which network?" Alice asked.

"Actually, they're Russians," Melanie said. "With a program called *600 Seconds.*"

"I've heard of that," Alice said.

Grace knew her daughter probably had heard of the Russian show, though she herself hadn't; her daughter, for all her typical teenage posturing, was a brilliant student who had a surprising grasp of current affairs, domestic and foreign.

"I'm sure you've made our guests feel at home," Grace said.

Melanie nodded her pretty head back toward the coach area of the ship. "I just gave their fearless leader his VIP press kit," she explained. "He's a handsome devil. . . . They'd like to have a few moments with the two of you. Would you mind?"

"Not right now," Grace said. "Maybe after we've had some sleep."

"Fine," Melanie said. "I'll check back."

As in a theater before the curtain goes up, the lights on the ship flickered. Out the windows the vehicles of Russian and American military guards were backing away as the sleeping giant of AFO came awake, its engines first purring, then roaring to life.

With takeoff imminent, Melanie took one of the first-class seats, across from Alice, and seat-belted herself in. The steward, Joey, arrived with the cocoa on a tray; the sight of the mound of whip cream on top seemed to improve Alice's mood. A slender attractive black woman, one of Grace's aides, approached, and the First Lady rose and spoke with her about the next day's schedule while Alice used a spoon to nibble at the whip cream.

The plane jolted forward, beginning to taxi.

Leaning forward in the comfortable chair, Alice looked up, toward the presidential stateroom; would her father miss his cue?

The door opened, and the President of the United States of America emerged, looking casual with the sleeves of his shirt rolled up, tie loose, suit coat left behind. As he frequently did, he was checking his wristwatch.

Still looking at the watch, he said, "You guys back already?"

Alice looked at her mother with smug self-satisfaction.

"Hi, hon," Jim said, and gave Grace—still standing with her aide—a peck of a kiss. Looking toward his daughter, he said, "How was the ballet?"

"Bolshoi," Alice said.

A wry little smile dug into her father's cheek. "I hope that wasn't a pun."

Chief of Staff Lloyd Shepherd came up the hallway, papers in hand, saying, "Mr. President—they're ready for you in the conference room."

"Go on, Shep," Jim said. "I'll be along in a few minutes."

That was a break from standard operating procedure, and Shep seemed as surprised as Grace and Alice.

"But Mr. President . . ." Shep began.

"I'll be along," Jim said sharply.

And Shepherd nodded, turned tail, and went away.

Jim settled into the first-class seat beside his daughter. As pleasant as that sight was, Grace was concerned; Jim just didn't keep a staff meeting on hold to spend a little time with his family.

"Is something wrong, dear?" she asked him, standing beside where he sat.

He looked up at her. "Terribly wrong," he said. "I just realized I've barely seen either of you, all week."

Though the plane was still taxiing, Melanie Mitchell was unstrapping herself, getting up; Grace was just thinking about how nice it was of the young woman to go away and give them some privacy when the deputy press secretary said, "Excuse me, I'm going to go get a photographer. . . ."

Apparently the President wasn't the only one who had noticed he and his family hadn't been seen together all week; to Melanie Mitchell, this was a photo op.

"No, Ms. Mitchell," Jim said, not crossly. "Give us a few moments alone, would you?"

Embarrassed, Melanie said, "Yes, Mr. President," and disappeared down the hall.

"Dad," Alice asked, "you don't have a fever or anything? You didn't catch the Russian flu and are going loopy on us, are you?"

"Actually," he said, taking his daughter's hand, "I haven't felt this good in a long time. Was Pavlova dancing tonight?"

Alice glowed; she reached forward for the slippers and displayed the autograph for her father.

"Wow," he said, examining the dainty shoes. "These'll come in handy for dance class. . . ."

Laughing, Alice took the precious shoes back. "I remember you. You used to be my dad."

"I remember you, too. You used to fit in the crook of my arm and my palm. . . ."

He took his daughter into his arms. "I'm sorry, angel. I've been neglecting you guys terribly."

As they drew apart, Alice said, "You've been working yourself too hard. You owe it to yourself, Dad, to take a little time. You owe it to the country!"

That made him laugh, and he said, "I know some people who would like to see me take a *lot* of time off—they're called Democrats."

Grace, standing nearby, said, "We understand, dear."

Jim looked from his daughter to his wife and back again. "No. No, there's no excuse for the way I've been putting you guys off. Not even if I were the President of the United States . . ."

Alice's smile was a wonder. "You *are* the President of the United States."

"Oh, yeah, that's right, I forgot! You know what that means? There's this resort I can take you two to . . . called Camp David. . . ."

"I know that resort," Alice said. "It's full of advisers and ambassadors and your chief of staff."

"Not this time. I'm gonna clear a weekend sometime this month. I promise."

"Is that a real promise," Alice asked, "or a campaign promise?"

He gave her a hard look. "You know, most parents have to restrict their kids from watching too much MTV. Me, I have to keep you away from the damn McLaughlin Group!"

Alice laughed, and so did Grace, who leaned in and whispered gently, "I know you have that conference . . . but I need a minute. Alone."

"Sure, honey," he said, and patted his daughter's hand, then rose and took Grace's hand.

She led him to their stateroom, where they slipped inside and she kissed him on the mouth; not a peck. She wanted her man to know just how she loved him, and he responded with the urgency she knew so well. It was good to know he was as hungry for her as she was for him.

But somehow he read it a little wrong, because—with

her still in his arms—he gazed at her, troubled, saying, "What's the matter?"

"What?"

He drew away. "Something's on your mind."

He knew her so well; she'd never been able to hide a thing from him—not that he could ever hide anything from her.

"I heard your speech," Grace said. "They were replaying it on the radio. We heard it in the limo on the way from the ballet."

He sighed, and dropped himself to the couch, sitting there, looking glum, suddenly. "Political suicide, huh? Please don't scold me.... I'm getting enough of that from Shep and Jack."

She sat beside him, took one of his hands in both of hers. "No, no ... I'm proud of you. You did the right thing. The only thing you could do."

He seemed startled by this approval. "You're the only one who thinks so."

"That night you won New Hampshire ..."

He blinked. "New Hampshire? What brought this on?"

"The night you won New Hampshire, I was so proud, so ... relieved."

"Relieved?"

She nodded. "That the country had come to its senses, that this country had a chance now, because they'd seen in you what I saw in you, from the very beginning."

"What did you see?"

"A hero."

He laughed a little. "Haven't you heard? My war record has been grossly exaggerated; it was in all the papers."

"That's not the kind of hero I mean. I'm talking about somebody who can withstand all the pressures and temptations and can still keep a fix on what's important, and what he believes in."

"You think I've managed that?"

"Not entirely . . . You've compromised, like every politician does sooner or later."

He sighed. "Sometimes it seems like all our energy goes into just trying to survive. Sometimes I think we're spending this entire term with our eye on making sure we get another goddamn term."

"I know. I know. But tonight . . . tonight when you gave that speech, I felt the way I did in New Hampshire. Very much the same way."

"Really?"

"Really. It was like . . . like you suddenly remembered why you wanted this job in the first place."

He looked at her a long time, and then he kissed her. The kiss was getting very interesting when the knock— the dreaded knock—came at the door.

"Mr. President?"

Shep's voice.

He looked at her, sighed, shrugged, and she nodded her permission; duty was duty.

She touched his face. "I just wanted you to know, dear, no matter what your advisers tell you, no matter what the media or your opposition says about you . . . I'm proud of the stand you took tonight. . . . It reminded me of somebody very special."

"Who?"

"You."

She gave him a peck, and sent him on his way, then returned to the lounge area to gather her daughter up. This ship was a second home to them, after all, and it would be bedtime, soon.

*Chapter Six*_____

Within the cockpit of Air Force One, Colonel Gregory Axelrod and his copilot, Lieutenant Colonel Arthur Ingrahams, sat in the glow of the red and blue and green lights of their controls, waiting for clearance, the chiseled features of Ingrahams, black, a Desert Storm vet, thrown into dramatic relief. Axelrod had flown with Ingrahams for over two years and could not ask for a better second chair. Behind them, hunkered over the central console, the flight-engineer panel lights winking at him, sat their navigator, Major Daniel Ballard, pale, mustached, pleasant, also a Desert Storm vet.

The three men shared the same voice in their headsets: "Tower to United States Air Force One." The voice was crisply Russian, accented but in full command of English. "It's an honor to clear you for immediate takeoff on runway three."

"Roger, Tower," Axelrod said. "Thank you for the hospitality."

And the President's pilot eased up on the throttle, bringing the four GE-F103 turbofan engines to life.

Soon the press and the dignitaries on the ground, and the Russian citizens who'd gathered to witness the finish of this historic trip, were rewarded with a picture-perfect takeoff as Air Force One glided off the runway and into the night sky, sliding through the moonlight, skating upward on its sheet of air.

Before long it was gone, with only the clouds below and the stars above to watch its effortless flight through the midnight sky. If God were watching—and, of course, in the beliefs of many, God is always watching—He might enjoy the tranquillity of the sight of a sleek yet monstrous man-made mechanism of flight, sailing His skies with a grace to rival any bird.

But if God were watching, He would also be aware that there was a traitor aboard Air Force One.

Just past midnight on AFO, drowsiness had overtaken much of the plane. Lulled by the drone of the engines, many passengers and aides were asleep, their leather first-class chairs leaned back, blankets and little pillows in use; a few of the overhead TVs were going, for the benefit of night owls and news junkies.

A CNN reporter was reporting on President Marshall's antiterrorism speech, and the latest developments in Kazakhstan, where the neo-Communist movement was floundering in the wake of General Radek's seizure "in the joint military action" undertaken by the United States and Russia, which had dealt a "major blow to the movement to unify the former Soviet Union, which had been gaining momentum in several ex-Soviet republics over the past year and until recently threatened to ignite a Russian civil war."

In the rear galley, Joey Elsner, the steward assigned specifically to baby-sit the needs of the President and the

First Family, was pouring coffee into mugs emblazoned with the same seal of state that appeared on Joey's apron. No paper cups for the prez and his kin . . .

"The administration has been calling the act 'a onetime intervention,'" the CNN reporter was saying, "but the President's speech alluded to a major change in U.S. foreign policy."

Joey, with a tray of half a dozen mugs of coffee, moved past the private cabins; he paused at the door to the President's office. Knocked lightly.

The First Lady answered with a quiet, "Yes?", and Joey said, "Your coffee, Mrs. Marshall," and she bid him come in.

Having abandoned her gown for a yellow cashmere sweater and black slacks, she was sitting at the President's desk—the only other person on earth (or above it) who dared sit there—signing some letters a secretary had typed up for her. Joey served the coffee (he'd already added cream in the galley) and glanced toward the presidential stateroom.

"No more cocoa tonight?" he asked.

"No more cocoa tonight," the First Lady said with a mild little smile. "She fell asleep watching CNN. I tucked her in a few minutes ago. . . . Thanks for your kindness to her, Joey."

"Alice is a nice kid, Mrs. Marshall."

"Yes she is. Even though you sometimes have to look close to tell."

Joey took his leave and headed down the hallway, past various slumbering aides; here and there, Secret Service agents had eased their vigil only to the point of sitting down. The Secret Service never slept. Like Joey.

He didn't bother to knock at the conference-room door; they were expecting him, and besides, for a knock to be heard in the sound-shielded room, he'd about have to use a sledgehammer. Joey was the only steward on AFO cleared to come and go, like this, in the conference room; he was proud of that fact—he liked to think of himself as the presidential steward, though that title existed only in his mind.

Coffee tray in one hand, Joey shut the conference-room door with the other; the soundproof room kept even the engine drone out. Right now the lights were dimmed as solemn-faced Major Norman Caldwell, a military adviser who was a frequent AFO guest, projected satellite photos onto a screen.

Joey, whose impeccable security clearance was in part due to his complete lack of knowledge and understanding of world affairs, did not recognize the projected photos as satellite views of Iraqi military bases.

"Our KH-11s took this one at 0100 hours, sir," Major Caldwell was saying to the President, who was seated at the smallish conference table with Mr. Doherty and Mr. Shepherd. "What you see here is the mobilization of two mechanized brigades toward Kurdish positions."

Joey was serving the President's coffee.

President Marshall asked, "What's the word from State?"

Doherty said, "The Iraqi ambassador is claiming it's just an 'exercise.'"

"That doesn't look like Richard Simmons to me," Marshall said, pointing at the screen. "Don't waste any time—send the *Nimitz* back in."

Joey was serving Doherty now; it was exciting, being a

fly on the wall while history was made—of course, he didn't understand any of this, but what he overheard always sounded so important.

"The northern border's gotten pretty hairy," Major Caldwell said. "Their MiGs are playing tag with our Falcons and our boys are getting itchy to engage. . . ."

"No Wild West show," Marshall said. "They only fire when fired upon. Make that clear! I don't need them creating policy for me."

"You don't need any help on that score," Doherty observed dryly.

Marshall gave Doherty a sharp look, but then the two men smiled at each other and laughed softly.

"Speaking of which," Marshall said, "do we have an update on the Kazakhstan elections?"

And Joey, having served coffee all around, slipped back out into the hallway, shutting the conference room back into its soundproof cocoon, a single black coffee remaining on his tray. A man in a perfectly pressed suit and tie, passing by, lifted the final coffee mug off Joey's tray, without a word.

The man's face was buried in some paperwork, but Joey knew him, all right. One of those uptight Secret Service assholes, typically cold, arrogantly rude.

What Joey didn't know was that his last cup of coffee had just gone to the traitor on Air Force One.

The Traitor had, in his hands, three photocopies of a report that had just come in over the fax in the in-flight office; he'd made the copies himself, to thoughtfully share with his fellow agents.

He stepped into the Secret Service cabin, where the

lights were dim and the three agents lounged back in their comfy leather first-class seats, taking it easy but staving off sleep. The Secret Service, after all, never slept.

Shutting the door behind him, the Traitor said, "We got the advance report on Miami. Who's interested?"

Everybody made noises to the effect of, yeah, sure, hand 'em out.

"Don't get up, guys," the Traitor kidded them.

And he went to them, where they sat, passing around with one hand (coffee cup in the other) the photocopies like menus to his colleagues: Cummins, blond, a former fullback from USC; Jackson, black, lean, Phi Beta Kappa, Drake University; and Napier, pale, brown-haired . . . where had he gone to school? The Traitor couldn't remember.

What he did remember, as he sipped his coffee, was that he knew these men, had worked with these men, and it was a damn shame they had to die so that he could be wealthy.

But they weren't as important as he was, were they?

And, so, as the finely tuned, precisely trained agents, men trained as detectives, schooled as bodyguards, the elite in their field of investigation and protection, looked at the advance report handed to them by a trusted fellow agent, that fellow agent—the Traitor aboard Air Force One—calmly withdrew his noise-suppressed nine millimeter from under a suit coat especially tailored to conceal the rather bulky weapon and, one at time, in rapid succession, shot Cummins, Jackson, and Napier in their heads.

And, for once, the Secret Service slept.

Like Kennedy, he thought, *they never knew what hit them.*

He hoped he would go the same way, that the same favor would one day be done him: no warning, no suffering. Just a quick lights-out and on to the next world, if there was one.

The three dead men in the tilted-back leather first-class seats sat watching nothing, their dead eyes still on the reports in their slack hands, blood spattering the photocopies, and streaming down the creases of their leather chairs.

Had their eyes not been sightless, they might have seen their former colleague, silenced nine millimeter in hand, poised near the closed door, listening. Not that the murders of these three men had created much of a stir, but "silenced" gunshots are not really silent, and someone might have heard the slight commotion as the three skulls cracked from a gunshot, three bodies jerked in leather seats. . . .

But the plane, like Cummins, Jackson, and Napier, slept. Only the drone of engines accompanied the Traitor's actions as he returned his automatic to its special shoulder rig, withdrew a key from his pocket and, as casually as if he were at the front door of his home, inserted the key into an alarm-style lock on the wall, a small panel sliding back to reveal a touch pad. Sipping his coffee, he used his free hand to tap in a series of numbers.

With those numbers entered, a click signaled the unlocking of the arms cabinet. The Traitor slid back the hidden panel, revealing the recessed locker that contained many weapons but from which the Traitor withdrew only one item: a smoke grenade.

After a final sip of coffee, the Traitor pulled the pin on the grenade and rolled it across the room as he went to the door and coolly exited, heading toward the front of the plane, leaving the door slightly ajar, which might seem a peculiar thing to do, at the scene of a multiple murder.

But the Traitor was out of sight by the time the thick white smoke began billowing out that ajar door, fluffy friendly clouds drifting by slumbering staffers, at first, and then people began to stir and wake up and cough and notice. . . .

And the ship was suddenly awake, and shouts and even screams soon made it clear that the consensus was *the plane's on fire!*

The smoke found its way to the rear cabin, where the press and various lesser governmental minions rode coach, but most everyone back there was asleep when the white clouds began to form.

One man, however, was expecting this change in the weather.

Actually, six were. But one man in particular had been waiting, their leader, Korshunov, only that wasn't his real name, just as he wasn't really a producer with the program *600 Seconds*.

He moved quickly past the rear galley and down the aisle as those around him were beginning to rouse, and moved into the Secret Service cabin, through that ajar door, charging into the source of the dense, choking smoke, like a courageous fireman seeking a child in a burning house.

Only Korshunov was seeking something else: that open panel where the unlocked arms locker held enough weaponry to start a small war, which, not coincidentally, was Korshunov's aim, more or less. Holding his breath as smoke streamed around him, he helped himself to the goodies within the Secret Service locker, machine pistols, assault vests, smoke grenades. . . .

Out in the hallway, a Secret Service agent named Landon Pardy was moving through excited, near-panicking staffers toward the smoke that billowed from the Secret Service cabin.

Thinking he was dealing with a fire, Pardy pushed open the cabin door and, poised in the doorway, saw, through the haze of white, his three fellow agents, leaned back comfortably in their leather chairs, skulls shattered, trickles of blood streamed down over their dead empty faces.

Expert training was not enough to save him. The stunned second it took Pardy to register the hazy sight of his dead colleagues was followed by the realization that the Russian TV journalist Korshunov was at the arms locker, helping himself, and as Pardy went for his shoulder-holstered weapon, Korshunov ripped off a precise burst of automatic fire from a machine pistol.

The dead Pardy toppled out into the hallway, more smoke pouring out after him, and an air-force security guard named Davis, hearing shots followed by the blood-spattered body of Pardy tumbling from the cabin, back-pedaled down the hall, scurrying to the forward portion of the plane, to seek reinforcements and send word to secure the President.

But Secret Service Agent Walters, in a forward lounge area, had already heard the shots and reacted immediately, grabbing a wall intercom phone even as he was withdrawing his weapon.

"Shots fired!" Walters shouted into the intercom. "Secure Boy Scout! Shots fired!"

Gunfire was popping down the corridor, short firecracker bursts promising worse things to come. Air Force Security Guard Davis had come into Walters's view; Davis took position by the conference-room door even as the Secret Service agent outside the stateroom pulled his weapon and dropped into firing position. Secret Service Agent Gibbs, back by the forward galley getting some coffee, drew his belt-holstered revolver and took position there, crouching, stealing glances down the corridor. This was where Joey the steward was also crouching, his attitude toward the Secret Service getting adjusted.

By this time the other self-proclaimed Kazakhstan freedom fighters (who'd been posing as the *600 Seconds* news crew) had slung themselves into assault vests, courtesy of the Secret Service arms locker.

One of Korshunov's freedom fighters, Vladimir Krasin— tall, dark, pockmarked—had returned to the coach cabin where he'd previously been a quiet, well-behaved passenger and shouted, "Down! Down! Everybody down!", and as frightened staffers and reporters crouched in their seats, Krasin sent a burst of machine-pistol fire over their heads, to prove his resolve and demonstrate the bulletproof nature of the ship.

And in the main corridor, a full-scale firefight had broken out, with Korshunov and two of his men—blond, stocky Boris Bazylev and dark, brawny Andrei Kolchak— holding position, firing at Secret Service agents and airforce security guards down the hall.

Two other freedom fighters—lean, dead-eyed Sergei Lenski and fleshy, hook-nosed Igor Nevsky—had worked their way down to the in-flight office, where they burst in and found only one air-force security guard, whom Bazylev dropped with the butt of his machine pistol. Lenski disarmed the unconscious man, and the two freedom fighters joined their comrades in the corridor, who laid down cover as Lenski and Bazylev, keeping low, worked their way down the hall, diving into the indentation of a lounge area, which had been abandoned by staffers fleeing the now somewhat dissipated smoke of the initial grenade.

In the soundproofed conference room, it was as if none of this had happened.

The President of the United States, seated with three of his most trusted advisers, the Iraqi satellite photos still the largest looming problem, was saying, "Jack, bring Chapman up to date on this."

"Yes, sir," Doherty said.

"And call the ambassador. I don't want anybody left out of the loop."

And with that, the door burst open and Secret Service Agents Walters and Johnson, weapons drawn, barged in even as smoke and the sounds of gunfire swept across the startled conference room. Walters hit the light switch, flooding the room with illumination, as the President got immediately to his feet.

"What the hell's going on?" Marshall asked, even as Walters and Johnson were on top of him, lifting him off the ground in standard "human wall" Secret Service procedure.

"Shots fired, sir," Walters said matter-of-factly.

The sound of more shots being fired served as punctuation to his redundant statement.

"By who?" Marshall demanded. "Where's my family?"

"We're handling it, sir," Walters said as he and Johnson carried the President of the United States from the room, leaving Marshall's most trusted advisers to fend for themselves, to scramble out of the room in a cacophony of shouts.

And in the hallway, the Traitor—acting in his capacity as a loyal Secret Service agent—found his way to an intercom phone on a wall panel in the forward galley. He punched a red button and told the cockpit, "We have a code red, I repeat, code red. Shots fired onboard!"

Colonel Axelrod's voice came back: "Cabin/flight deck: code red acknowledged!"

And the Traitor, his duty to his president carried out, signed off, and took cover, as the bullets continued to fly.

*Chapter Seven*_____

In the cockpit of AFO, in the multicolor glow of his instrument panel, Colonel Axelrod, displaying that eerie calm only pilots can achieve in the face of disaster, summoned Maatstraight Control and declared an emergency.

In his headset, Axelrod heard the words of a Maatstraight navigator: "Nearest secure site is Ramstein Air Base."

The yoke of the 747 in his two hands as casually as if he were on a Sunday-afternoon drive, Axelrod said, "Bearing?"

"Two-seven-six, sir."

Axelrod quarter-turned to his copilot. "Get us a secure line."

Lieutenant Colonel Ingrahams toggled his headset switch.

"Dan," Axelrod said to their flight engineer, "is that door locked?"

"Already checked it, sir," Major Ballard said.

"Well, check it again."

Ballard did.

"Ramstein Tower," Ingrahams said, "this is Air Force

One Heavy. We have a code red, repeat, a code red. Shots fired onboard. Potus onboard."

Potus: President of the United States.

"Repeat," Ingrahams said, "shots fired, Potus onboard. Request emergency assistance. ETA . . ."

"Fifteen minutes," Ballard said.

"Fifteen minutes," Ingrahams repeated.

In their headsets, the crew of the Air Force One flight deck heard Ramstein's near-immediate response: "Air Force One, acknowledged. We have radar contact bearing zero-nine-six at eighty-two miles. Please state fuel remaining and souls onboard."

"Sixty-three souls onboard," Axelrod said. "Okay with fuel. Request secure military escort with emergency medical standing by. Potus and family aboard."

"Air Force One, acknowledged," the voice in their headsets said. "We are scrambling our fighters, repeat, we are scrambling our fighters. Emergency equipment will be standing by."

And in the air-traffic-control tower at the American air base at Ramstein, Germany, Air Force Major Theodore Hertel—Ramstein's supervisor of flying—peered over the shoulder of air-traffic-controller Lieutenant Gary Neibuhr, who was tracking the radar image of Air Force One. A once sleepy midnight control room had come alive, cranking into crisis mode.

"Wake the general," Hertel called out to the watch officer across the room, "now!"

And as his watch officer used the phone, rousing their commanding officer gently out of bed, Major Hertel made a ruder wake-up call to the entire base, hitting a red button on a console that sent sirens screeching and klaxons wailing. Above their control panels, the controllers and others on watch in the Ramstein tower could see out their angled windows the half a dozen pilots washed in moonlight, streaking across the runways toward their F-15 Eagles.

"General's on his way, sir."

"Call air traffic," Hertel told his watch officer. "Not a plane lands or takes off within two hundred miles. Understood?"

No answer was required.

On Air Force One, the daughter of the President—wearing the sweatshirt and jeans she'd fallen asleep in—was sitting bolt upright in the folded-out daybed of the presidential stateroom. Alice Marshall dreamed she heard shots. She *was* dreaming, wasn't she?

In the presidential office, Grace Marshall had fallen asleep at her husband's desk. She, too, sat up at the sounds; but she knew she wasn't dreaming. She knew she was hearing the wide-awake nightmare First Families could be forced to live through, at any given moment.

Grace jumped up from the desk, and moved quickly to the bathroom, which connected to the stateroom and her daughter. . . .

Only Alice had already moved to the stateroom door, and swung it open onto a smoke-filled hallway—was there a fire?—at the very moment her father was being swept along by the two Secret Service agents, like a victorious quarterback on the shoulders of his teammates.

Father's and daughter's eyes met, in mutual shock.

"Daddy!"

"Alice!"

But Agents Walters and Johnson ignored this touching family moment, carting their president toward the nearby front of the plane, where another Secret Service agent was positioned at the bottom of the winding stairway to the upper deck and the Missions Communications Center.

That agent, a very nice black man whose name Alice couldn't remember, came hurtling toward her, yelling, "Get back! Get back!"

He had almost reached her when a bullet crashed into, and through, his chest; and his wide-eyed expression was a horrible thing, as he collapsed, bumping into and blocking the door.

Alice didn't scream; she didn't even cover her mouth with one hand. She just sucked in air as she saw her father disappear, pulled back into the recession of the forward galley.

Agent Gibbs was peeking out from behind the galley divider, a revolver in hand, and he yelled, "Back, Alice! Get back!"

If that hadn't been enough to make her pull her head back in the stateroom, gunfire from down the hall was. She tried to push the door shut, but couldn't—that poor dead Secret Service agent, who'd tried to help her, was wedged there!

Then somebody grabbed her roughly from behind.

"Get back," her mother said.

Everyone was telling her that!

Then her mother was on hands and knees, reaching out for something—the dead agent's gun!

Grace snatched the automatic from the slack fingers, shoved the body into the hall, even as bullets whined and sang, putting her shoulder into the effort, finally shutting the door.

Getting to her feet, the dead agent's gun in her hand, Grace looked at her daughter, who looked at her, their eyes wide, mouths wide open, and they flew into each other's arms, and hugged, hugged desperately, while beyond the closed door the barely muffled sounds of gunfire played on, like some awful, violent television show someone was watching in the next room.

In the corridor beyond the stateroom, the smoke from the grenade was dissipating into a haze even as the gunfire increased. Behind and under the stairway to the Mission Communications Center, a trapdoor awaited, leading to the lower deck of AFO; this was the objective of the Secret Service agents who had carried their president forward.

But right now they were several frustrating feet away, pinned down in the forward galley, keeping the President behind a bulkhead. Secret Service Agent Gibbs and Air Force Security Guard Davis were taking turns laying a fusillade of handgun fire down the hallway, one firing, one reloading.

On the upper deck, in the Mission Communications Center—the sound of gunfire popping just beyond their door like some ghastly Fourth of July celebration—the trio of air-force specialists on duty were doing their best to fight panic, and get the word out.

"Yes," one of them was saying into his headset, "the Vice-President! Interrupt her. This is Air Force One with an emergency call. Potus at risk, repeat, Potus at risk!"

"General Greely, this is Air Force One," another was saying, "we have a code red. Shots have been fired."

In fact, shots were continually firing. In the forward galley below, Agent Johnson was returning fire down the smoky corridor, while Agent Walters leaned against the kitchen wall, using the intercom phone.

"All stations, all stations," he was saying, "we have secured Boy Scout, and we're going to the vault. Repeat, we are going to the vault."

Walters hung up, and looked down at his president, who scowled as he crouched behind the bulkhead. "Ready, sir?"

"What about my family?"

"Sir, it's time."

Walters and Johnson again formed a human barricade around the President, and Gibbs pivoted into the hallway, dropping into a crouch, providing cover, as Davis put himself between the terrorists down the corridor and the two-man human wall of Secret Service agents moving the President toward the upper-deck stairway.

Then Davis took one squarely in the chest and was dead before he hit the floor; another round nailed Johnson, in the shoulder, blood blossoming through his suit coat. The agent flinched but kept moving.

Marshall said, "Jesus!"

Working his voice above the gunfire, Johnson said, "This way, sir . . ."

And they moved the President behind the stairs and Agent Walters pulled up a floor panel that was all but invisible in the carpeting, revealing stairs descending into the forward rear galley.

"After you, sir," Walters said, and shoved the President into the stairwell.

*   *   *

In the AFO cockpit, Colonel Axelrod could hear the shots outside the flight-deck door.

"You think they've stormed the MCC yet?" Axelrod asked his copilot, referring to the Mission Communications Center on the other side of that door, just behind Major Ballard.

"I can check with them, sir, and find out," Ingrahams said.

"No," Axelrod said, "they have their hands full in any event."

Ingrahams grimaced. "Who the hell's doing this?"

"Maybe it's the Democrats," Axelrod said.

A voice in the headsets of the flight-deck crew said: "Air Force One, landing cleared for runway zero-nine."

"Roger," Ingrahams said. "Turning left to heading one-eight-five. Descending to flight level, two-zero-zero."

Gunfire kept popping out there, sounding far away—and yet so very close.

"You're sure about that door?" Axelrod asked Ballard.

"Oh yeah," Ballard said.

Axelrod banked the big plane into a curve, descending through broken clouds. Out the double windshield, they could see, in the pale moonlight, shiny streaks of metal bursting through those clouds.

The squadron of F-15 Eagles was rising into formation, around Air Force One. One hell of a sight.

Axelrod looked at Ingrahams and they traded smiles.

"Air Force One," a new voice in their headsets said, "this is Colonel Carlton, Halo flight leader. You are now under escort. All airspace has been cleared."

Outside the cockpit door, the crack of gunshots continued.

"This is Air Force One," Ingrahams said. "We're coming in hot. ETA to Ramstein—"

Ballard said, "Ten minutes."

"—ten minutes," Ingrahams finished.

The three men of the AFO flight-deck crew exchanged grim glances; those gunshots out there seemed much closer than just ten minutes away.

In the cockpit of his F-15 Eagle, USAF Colonel Frank Carlton—encased in helmet, mask, and visor—was thinking the same thing: he could see the gunfire flashes in the dark windows of the plane.

"Alert forces mobilized," Carlton informed the pilot of AFO. "Just get that bird on that ground."

"Roger," the voice of Colonel Ingrahams said in Carlton's headset, with a confidence that both men knew was entirely unwarranted.

Beneath the main cabin, on the lower deck of Air Force One, Walters and Johnson moved the President at a pace just short of a run through the lower front galley with its compartments, storage freezers, and food-preparation tables. On the far side of the galley, Walters flung open a hatchway and guided the President onto a rubber-floored gangway that ran from the lower galley into the rear baggage hold, flanked on either side by landing-gear bays. Walters and Johnson had traded sides on the President so that Johnson could use his good arm, as opposed to the one gushing blood.

Ducking under wing supports, the trio came to a mesh

grating, which Walter lifted, revealing the sleek, NASA lines of an escape pod.

"Sir," Walters said, swinging up the door for the one-man vehicle, "get in!"

Marshall froze. The cushioned seat within the rounded chamber did not call out to him; rather, it accused him: *coward. What am I,* he thought, *some James Bond villain escaping?*

"No fucking way," Marshall said. "This is my ship. . . ."

"Get in, sir," Johnson said; the man was almost woozy from blood loss. "Your ship is the ship of *state* . . . get in!"

And those words, fairly eloquent under the circumstances, were Johnson's last, as a burst of automatic gunfire, from down the gangway in the direction from which they'd come, ripped up the front of him, obliterating the intelligent features of his face, turning them into an explosion of blood mist and organic matter.

Marshall dove across the way, for cover, behind a wing strut; Walters had taken cover across the gangway, behind another wing strut, near the escape pod. The agent leaned out and returned fire, three quick rounds, quelling the volley, for the moment.

As Walters leaned back against the bulkhead, reloading, the agent said to his president, "On the count of three, sir, you're going for the pod."

"What about my family?"

"Johnson had a family," Walters said. The dead agent was sprawled on the gangway, red stripes of his blood streaming across his white shirt and blue suit. "And so do I. On the count of three, sir . . . Go for the goddamn pod!"

Marshall said, "I'll go for Johnson's gun. We can hold them off, you and I."

And a mechanical Bronx cheer of automatic gunfire came from down the gangway.

"Mr. President," Walters said. "Mr. President! You have to do this. . . . Ready?"

"No."

"One."

"No!"

"Two."

"No . . ."

"Three!"

And the agent combat-rolled into the open, onto the gangway, with the sprawled body of his dead colleague his only cover, shooting blindly, his only goal to serve as a shield for the President, giving Marshall the time he needed to dive behind the agent, toward the pod.

Moments before, furtively shown the way by the Traitor, Lenski and Bazylev—the two freedom fighters dispatched by Korshunov ("Get the President!")—had descended the metal stairs into the lower deck, moving through the galley hatchway onto the gangway.

Now, ducked behind a bulkhead on either side of the gangway, Lenski and Bazylev let rip with their MP-5s. The automatic gunfire punctured the agent's body, shook him, destroyed him.

And when the bullet-riddled body dropped like a side of beef to the gangway, flopping, splashing in its own blood, the mechanical whine of the pod sliding on its rails alerted the two freedom fighters to the success of the agent's effort and their own failure. The pod door was closing. . . .

Unleashing sprays of automatic gunfire, Lenski and Bazylev rushed down the gangway, but the bullets careened off the bulletproof surface of the pod like so many hailstones.

Then it was gone, out of their view, as the sleek NASA capsule accelerated along its rails, running the rest of the length of the plane, a signal strobing-flashing to alert the bay door ahead to open, which it did, the pod ejecting from the underbelly of the plane, its para-hook snapping a line.

From the cockpit, Colonel Axelrod, Lieutenant Colonel Ingrahams and Major Ballard could see it, the pod shooting out, clear of the plane, three large parachutes blooming, the pod gently descending to earth like the returning space capsule it resembled.

Had they not seen this glorious sight, the light flashing on the instrument panel would have reported the pod's progress.

And now it was up to Colonel Axelrod to pass the good news along: "Ramstein, this is Air Force One. . . . Emergency Pod has been deployed! I repeat, emergency pod has been deployed."

In their headsets, the flight crew heard: "Ramstein Tower acknowledging. We are picking up the beacon and deploying search and rescue."

Axelrod and Ingrahams exchanged grins; no matter how this came out, the bad guys (whoever the hell they were) had failed: the President was safe.

"Ramstein," Lieutenant Colonel Ingrahams said into

his headset, "we are descending to five thousand feet, beginning final approach. . . ."

And just outside the flight deck, gunshots were ringing the doorbell.

*Chapter Eight*_____

The Kazakhstan freedom fighters had complete control of the main deck, strutting down the aisles in their assault vests, machine pistols in hand, winding in and around and over the terrified Americans lying flat on the aircraft floor. Aides, secretaries, stewards hugged the carpet in the main corridor and in the recessions of lounge areas, scattered like corpses that hadn't gotten around to dying yet.

Korshunov had rounded up several Secret Service agents, among them Gibbs, who was bloody from Korshunov striking him in the face, and was herding them into the conference room. This distracted the other terrorists long enough for one of the helpless victims on the floor to inch forward another few feet.

Lieutenant Colonel Dewayne Perkins—the briefcase known as the nuclear football handcuffed to his wrist—was moving along on his belly as if he were ducking enemy gunfire in a war zone, and wasn't that exactly what he was doing?

Perkins had taken a round in his shoulder, and it hurt like a son-of-a-bitch, and as he crawled he left a red snaillike trail behind him; but he gritted his goddamn teeth and headed for his objective because he was a god-damn marine with a goddamn responsibility.

The goddamn responsibility chained to his wrist repre-sented the lives of millions; his life was pledged to pro-tect those countless faceless others, and it would be a small price to pay. If he lost his life before he could fulfill his duty, however, the price would be large indeed. . . .

"Everybody stay down!" one of the bastards was saying.

Gradually, as the terrorists stepped over him and his fellow hostages, Perkins worked his way toward the goal up ahead: the door to the in-flight office. A simple office machine could stave off an unimaginable disaster. And finally, the back of the nearest terrorist turned to him, Perkins—still crawling like a snake—edged open that office door and was slipping inside, when Nevsky spotted him, saying, "Hey!" and taking pursuit.

But the terrorist got a door shut and locked in his face, and the burly marine worked the combination on the black leather briefcase, as quickly as he could, even as bullets tore at the door lock.

The machine was switched on; the briefcase was open; the papers were in his hands.

But Nevsky was kicking in the door.

Perkins fed the sheets of paper into the machine, as behind him the door splintered open under Nevsky's boot. The marine whirled, his .45 automatic in one hand, the briefcase on its chain swinging from his left wrist like an absurd oversize cuff link, and Nevsky's MP-5 ripped across the front of Perkins, stitching across him and unstitching his insides at the same time.

But Perkins, dying a quick if excruciating death, went

out of this life with a smile, witnessing a beautiful sight: those papers, nuclear-war strategies, the SIOP (Single Integrated Operations Plan) booklet, missile launch codes, were feeding through the paper shredder, their confetti-like remains raining down over the expiring marine hero in a tickertape parade.

Stalking down the corridor, MP-5 in hand, Korshunov—annoyed that Lenski and Basylev had not yet returned from the baggage deck with the President—checked the presidential stateroom himself. Two important hostages were not among the cannon fodder hugging the floor elsewhere in the plane; to make the President, and his people, do as Korshunov commanded, the freedom fighters' leader would need the so-called First Family.

Kicking aside the corpse of a Secret Service agent blocking the way, Korshunov tried the presidential stateroom door; oddly, it was not locked. Perhaps mother and daughter had scurried out into some designated hiding place. If so, there would be a need to scour the plane for such insects.

Stepping inside, he found that the grenade smoke that had thinned in the hallway remained fairly thick in here; this door had been opened, at some point, for that smoke to have gotten in. So perhaps the First Lady and her precious little girl had in fact flown—

The shot slammed into the door, inches from his head. He dropped to the floor as two more rounds flew over his head and out the open doorway; then he rolled for cover as more rounds followed, missing him wildly, chewing up the bland furnishings in the presidential stateroom.

He'd snugged himself behind a chair when he realized the shots had stopped and the clicking he heard—and the heavy breathing, which was nearly sobbing—would indicate his foe was out of ammunition.

She had barricaded herself, and her child, behind a table. The gun in her hand—that of the dead Secret Service agent Korshunov had kicked aside, coming in, no doubt—remained aimed at him and impotently clicking on its empty chamber as Korshunov stood slowly, walking toward her, where she fired her empty gun, the eyes in that famous poised face as wild as any animal's.

And behind the wild animal was her cub, Alice, biting her fist, huddling there, shaking with fright—America's future.

Korshunov thought about slapping the woman—she had tried to kill him, after all—but he was a civilized man. He merely removed the gun from her hand, tossed it aside, and hauled her by the slender arm to her feet.

"Come," he said. "Join the party."

"What have you done with my daddy?" the girl demanded.

"Nothing," Korshunov said. "Yet."

And he pushed the two females in front of him and marched them down the corridor to the conference room, with the rest of the more important hostages.

Then he gathered Kolchak, the man this mission so hinged upon, for the next phase of their assault.

Soon, wearing the greenish patina of monitors, digital displays, and other control-panel glow, Korshunov and Kolchak were stepping over and around the blood-oozing bodies of the three air-force communications specialists scattered about the Mission Communications Center, a chair knocked over here, a dropped handgun there.

Reloading his MP-5, Korshunov frowned—the acrid cordite smell the MP-5 left in its wake was making him nauseous, but the thirty-round German-made machine pistol with its collapsible stock was certainly a fine weapon. He had been able to fire single rounds and managed not to damage any of the high-tech equipment in this sizable control room.

The two men moved to the steel hatch to the flight deck; Korshunov tried to open it, found it locked, and began to pound like a frustrated suitor at his beloved's door.

"Let me in!" Korshunov cried. "You don't have to die!"

Within the cockpit, the pounding reverberated, like a bizarre kettledrum accompaniment to Korshunov's muffled grotesque love song ("I don't want to kill you!").

Colonel Axelrod, Lieutenant Colonel Ingrahams, and their navigator, Major Ballard, ignored the pounding, or pretended to. Up ahead was a reassuring sight: through the cockpit window, they could see, cutting a bright wedge between German towns and fields, the glowing landing lights of Ramstein Air Base.

"Ramstein Tower," Ingrahams said into his headset, "we are one-five miles coming in red-hot!"

And in their headsets came: "Roger, Air Force One. Wind is zero-niner-zero at one-two. You are cleared to land."

Down on the Ramstein airfield, rescue vehicles rolled into position, sirens wailing, while snipers carrying high-powered rifles with infrared scopes took positions atop rescue vehicles, barracks, and the control tower itself. The blades of a helicopter stirred the night as it descended to a runway, where it had barely alighted when a dozen heavily armed Special Forces troops leaped out and charged to waiting flatbed trucks.

Plunging over the city, the plane sprouted its landing gear, coming in fast and low. Soon the navigation lights of Air Force One were visible to those on the ground, the ship materializing out of darkness, escorted by the battery of F-15s, which then pulled away, like the grand finale of an air show.

Aboard the descending ship, Korshunov let his MP-5 rip across the flight-deck door; nickel-size indentations kissed the steel surface, bullets ricocheted and careened, the two freedom fighters covering their faces, swearing in Russian. Within the cockpit, the dull thuds of the bullets hitting had been like an ominous knocking at their door. The worst sort of company was about to arrive.

"Artie," Axelrod said, with a grim glance at his co-pilot, "no matter happens, we land this sucker. Understood?"

"Yes, sir," Ingrahams said.

The two men's eyes locked in a final contract.

"Gear down," Axelrod said.

On the other side of the cockpit door, another order was issued by a commanding officer.

"C-4," Korshunov said.

Kolchak withdrew a small canister from his assault vest, handed it to Korshunov, who secured a thumb-size amount of the plastic explosive, which he proceeded to wad about the hatch door.

"Blasting cap," Korshunov said, a surgeon asking for the next instrument.

Kolchak handed him the blasting cap, which Korshunov shoved into the wad of C-4.

Within the cockpit, Axelrod was lowering his flaps, saying, "Come on, baby . . . almost there," the landing strip so close he could touch it, airspeed, altitude dropping. "Flaps thirty . . ."

Three hundred feet . . . two hundred feet . . .

The three men who comprised the flight-deck crew of Air Force One stole small self-satisfied glances as they moved in on the final approach. They had beaten the odds. The wolves at the door had been held at bay.

Fifty feet . . . forty feet . . . thirty feet . . .

AFO's tires were hovering above the ground, as all of Ramstein airfield held its collective breath, and just as the great ship's wheels touched the runway, Ivan Korshunov fired a single MP-5 round into the blasting cap, exploding the door off its hinges in a blinding flash, instantly killing Major Ballard.

The wheels of AFO bounced off the runway, even as Korshunov and Kolchak burst in with the stench and smoke of the explosion, shoving aside the slumped-over scorched corpse of the flight engineer. The Russians moved into classic skyjacker position as Axelrod and Ingrahams frantically tried to regain control of their instruments.

"Take us up!" Korshunov commanded, his machine pistol at the side of Axelrod's head, its nose against his headset earpiece. Kolchak had the copilot covered the same way.

Axelrod said nothing; his jaw was tightly set, his eyes on the beckoning Ramstein runway ahead. He was setting the wheels of AFO back on the ground when a single close-range shot from Korshunov's MP-5 fragmented the pilot's skull and splashed much of what used to be in it onto the windshield.

"Pull up or die!" Korshunov shouted at Ingrahams, who now had two machine pistols trained upon him.

But Ingrahams throttled down, all the way down, and the engines of Air Force One died. Then, with a single round from Kolchak's weapon, so did Ingrahams, slumping over the wheel.

Without the help of its dead flight crew, Air Force One taxied down the runway, passing the emergency vehicles and flatbeds of Special Forces, veering to the right now, cutting across runways toward the control tower, a truck swerving wildly to avoid collision with the careening plane.

And on that plane, in the conference room where the key hostages were gathered, Grace and Alice Marshall and some of the President's most valued advisers were shaken like dice and rolled from their chairs, slamming around, bouncing into each other. Their captors, however, lost neither their weapons nor their control of the situation.

In the cockpit, Korshunov was yanking the corpse of Colonel Axelrod from the captain's seat, yelling, "Come on! Come on!" to his fellow freedom fighter, who was between the seats, the dead Ingrahams nudging Kolchak, as if prompting him, as Kolchak took the throttle all the way up. Beyond the windshield, where the stain of the dead Axelrod's blood and brains was like some grotesque squashed bug that had somehow found its way to the wrong side of the glass, a surrealistic swirl of spotlights and gyrating flashing red lights combined with the screams of sirens and clanging of alarm bells, joining with the smoke-scorched air and trio of corpses to make the flight deck a cubicle in hell.

Air Force One lurched past the control tower, in which pandemonium reigned, the controller in charge shouting ambiguously, "We're losing it!", the big plane not slowing, a pair of Jeeps peeling off to avoid being crushed.

On the flight deck, the two living men having shoved the three dead ones aside, Kolchak was settling into the pilot's seat, getting his hands on the wheel. Korshunov patted his second-in-command on the shoulder, knowing with the ship in the hands of a pilot as experienced as Andrei Kolchak, victory would soon be snatched from . . .

And looming before them on the runway, directly in their path, sitting silently like a grand statue to aviation, was a monstrous plane, which experienced-pilot Kolchak immediately recognized as a C-141 Starlifter.

"Hang on!" Kolchak shouted, and he eased back on the wheel.

Air Force One, having been put through paces the smallest plane would balk at, responded sluggishly, its nose creeping stubbornly upward, even as it continued closing in on the Starlifter.

"We're not going to make it," Kolchak said.

"Yes we are," Korshunov said, and squeezed his comrade's shoulder.

"We're too close," Kolchak said. "I have to risk stalling her out. . . ."

Kolchak pulled back on the stick.

Like an injured bird struggling off the ground, its straining metal defying gravity, Air Force One barely cleared the Starlifter, the edge of her wing just missing the top of the other plane's tail, leaving a slightly ramshackle Ramstein rudely behind. The swarm of sharpshooters, emergency crews, and Special Forces could do nothing more than watch her rise majestically and disappear into the moonswept night.

Soon the escort of F-15s had regrouped around Air Force One, which was flying under a new captain: Andrei Kolchak.

"Thirty thousand feet," Kolchak said, wiping sweat from his brow, checking his instruments as best a one-man crew could manage. "Heading one-one-zero."

With professional ease, Kolchak banked the plane into a curve and activated the autopilot. Sighing heavily, he rose from the seat and said, "We're heading home."

Korshunov rose, grinning, and hugged his comrade, a genuine Russian bear hug.

Then, still smiling, said, "Haul these bodies out of here. Pile them just outside in that control room, for now. . . . I'll put Nevsky in charge of finding a cabin to stack the casualties in."

Kolchak nodded and, as his leader exited, began carting the corpses of the flight crew out of the cockpit, dragging these dead brave men like potato sacks.

Korshunov moved through the Mission Communications Center, stepping around the dead, exiting and going down the short winding flight of stairs onto the main deck, where his comrades were rounding up the rest of the survivors, who moved along with hands on heads, looking shell-shocked.

A snort of a laugh issued from Korshunov's lips. Americans were a pampered lot; war was always something fought on someone else's soil.

"I thought we should keep all the hostages together," Nevsky said. "In one place."

"Very good," Korshunov said. He liked his men to take initiative— within reason. "Where is he?"

Nevsky swallowed; almost innocently, he asked, "Who?"

"Solzhenitsyn, who do you think? The President!"

"Sir," Nevsky said, "the President is no longer on board."

"What?"

"He made his way to an escape pod."

Korshunov grabbed Nevsky by the shirtfront, then hurled him aside, cursing in Russian, but was already onto his next move, the next most valuable hostages on his list.

Marshall's family—the mother who so bravely shot at him, and her sniveling privileged brat. They weren't the President, but they would have to do.

*Chapter Nine*_____

Time of year didn't matter: the White House lawn remained an immaculately landscaped emerald expanse, its grass kept green in a similar manner, one might suppose, to President Reagan's hair staying black. As this late-fall afternoon settled into the first magic moments of dusk, the majestic American symbol that was the White House casting a cool blue shadow, a marine helicopter thundered in to touch gingerly down, and then, stepping from the chopper with the confidence of a commando, so did Kathryn Bennett.

Slender, with a patrician beauty some might call handsome, her ice-blond hair in a short stylish coif, Bennett moved quickly away from the copter, whose blades still churned the cool air; she wore no coat, the skirt of her gray business suit flapping above attractive legs that might have been a dancer's, but in fact belonged to the Vice-President of the United States of America.

Bennett was met by Thomas Lee, heavyset, dependable deputy national security adviser, his face tight with worry; behind him, as they crossed the lawn to Bennett, was a phalanx of advisers.

"Madame Vice-President," Lee said, "if you'll follow me, we can avoid the press."

Bennett was not the follower in this group, however, and when she came up even with them, she did not break stride, Lee and his little army having to retreat to turn and fall back in line with her. She was already moving through the double doors into the White House.

"I understand the escape pod was triggered," Bennett said. She had the gently melodic, well-modulated voice of a good trial attorney, which (before she had become a U.S. representative from a district in New Jersey) was precisely what she'd been. "Has the President been secured?"

Footsteps echoed down the South Corridor like gunshots.

"Not yet, Madame Vice-President," Lee said. "But the recovery team should have him very soon."

"Thank God. What about Air Force One?"

"We're in communication with Ramstein tower," Lee said. "They have visual contact—the plane was coming into the runaway when I was called away to meet you."

"So it should be on the ground by now."

"Yes, Madame Vice-President. And that will give us a lot of options to choose from."

They turned a corner, moving down a corridor in a blur, gunshot footsteps building to a volley.

She asked, "Do we have any idea yet who's responsible?"

Lee shook his head no. "All we know is that shots were fired; AFO is apparently in state of siege."

"How the hell could this happen?" Bennett demanded. "How the hell could anyone take over Air Force One?"

Lee extended his open palms in surrender. "We have no idea—this fits no known scenario we've ever run, no contingency we've ever planned for."

"That's reassuring."

"We don't know who we're dealing with or what they

want. No demands, no contact as yet, with whoever's done this . . ."

"With the First Lady and Alice aboard," Bennett said, "we could have a hostage situation the likes of which this country has never seen."

"No doubt about it, ma'am. But General Northwood assures me he has Special Forces poised for attack, the moment that plane touches down—just waiting for the go-ahead."

The words hit her hard, but she didn't break her stride; she merely frowned as mildly as if a waiter had informed her the special of the day was no longer available. "*My* go-ahead, you mean."

Lee's smile was nervous. "I think, in, uh, your absence, Mr. Dean will probably make that call, if he hasn't already. . . ."

Walter Dean was the secretary of defense; there was no love lost between the Vice-President—who viewed herself as tough yet compassionate—and the coldly logical Dean.

"If we're as close to making contact with the President as you say," Bennett said, "perhaps we ought to wait for him."

"According to Mr. Dean, the action will be over by the time we do."

"The 'action,'" Bennett said, and her frown deepened, and her stride approached a run. "You mean, commandos rushing aboard Air Force One with assault weapons to shoot it out over the heads of the President's wife, daughter, and forty or fifty White House staffers and representatives of the media?"

Lee had no answer to that.

And when the Vice-President, the national security adviser, and their entourage entered the Situation Room—where the walls were alive with the electronic glow of giant viewscreen maps and communications systems—all hell had broken loose. The men and handful of women who comprised this high-powered mix of civilian staff and military personnel, some at consoles around the periphery, the majority seated around an austere central conference table with individual laptops and secure telephones, were talking over and on top of each other like a family dinner that had turned ugly.

"What the hell is going on?" Bennett demanded, striding to the chair at the head of the table.

The room fell silent except for the sound of Teletype machines spitting out classified updates. The men and women at the table began to rise, but she waved them off impatiently. "Keep your seats, keep your seats. . . ."

"Madame Vice-President," Secretary of State Walter Dean said, and he twitched a thin, sickly smile, then his countenance turned dour as he sat back in his chair, arms folded. Seated at her left hand, Dean was a small, compact man, his short brown hair temple-touched with gray, his eyes hooded, remote.

Leaning forward in his chair was General William Northwood, U.S. Army, beefy, square-jawed, with surprisingly kind eyes—he might have been a dockworker, but he was the chair of the joint chiefs of staff.

Somber, General Northwood said to his vice-president, "Ma'am, Ramstein reports Air Force One is still airborne."

She had barely settled into her seat. "What?"

General Northwood sighed. "Apparently the plane touched down at Ramstein, and . . . took off again."

"Christ."

The big man gestured with one helpless hand. "Prior to that, the flight crew of AFO was maintaining radio contact with Ramstein . . . something that might have been an explosion in the cockpit was heard—"

"Explosion in the cockpit?" The Vice-President shook her head. "Are they dead? Who was in the cockpit, Colonel Axelrod and Lieutenant Colonel Ingrahams?"

She knew them well from her own many trips on AFO.

Northwood nodded glumly. "And Major Ballard. We don't know their status, ma'am. We do know they are no longer answering their radio."

"Dear God," Bennett said.

Air Force General Samuel Greely, an alert knife blade of a man in his late fifties, spoke up. "Our F-15 escort is keeping Air Force One in constant visual contact."

"What do they report?" she asked. "Who the hell is flying the plane?"

Greely raised an eyebrow. "An unidentified male civilian, ma'am . . . when there's anyone in the cockpit at all. Apparently the plane is on autopilot."

Dean, still sitting back, was drumming the eraser end of a pencil on the tabletop; otherwise he seemed spookily calm. He asked, "What are our airborne rescue scenarios?"

Greely's face tightened. "Airborne rescue scenarios? You mean, for dealing with terrorists who've skyjacked Air Force One? We don't have any."

Dean's smile was acid. "Then we'd better get some, General, don't you think? And they better be damn good, because we're not going to be running a hypothetical here, are we? Whatever you come up with, General, we'll be trying out in the field. Or should I say, sky?"

"How long can they stay up there," Bennett asked, "with the fuel they have?"

Northwood shrugged. "Well, that's a function of air-speed, wind—"

"Altitude," Greely added.

"Let's get another of the Air Force One pilots in here, ASAP," Bennett said. "Call Colonel Jackson in—let's get his take on it."

Nods around the table—except for Dean, who was eyeing her like a cobra about to bite. Greely was making the phone call to summon AFO's backup pilot.

"Any educated guesses," Bennett asked, "as to where this little charter is headed?"

Seated near her, Lee said, "Iraq, Libya, Algeria maybe . . ."

"Those are guesses, all right," Dean observed patroniz-ingly. "But I don't know if I'd call them 'educated.' Let's keep in mind the President's Moscow speech, shall we?"

"Kazakhstan?" Bennett mused.

And around the table, nods and shrugs affirmed this as the best possibility ventured thus far.

"Well," Bennett said, with a sigh, "I think it's time to notify the Allies." She turned to the security adviser. "Tom, can we keep this under wraps?"

"For now," Lee said. "We'll certainly do our best. But this kind of thing doesn't stay quiet very long."

Dean leaned near her and patted her hand. "Just try to relax, Kathryn," he near-whispered. "I'm in charge."

The Vice-President gave Dean a smile so condescend-ing it was worthy of Dean himself.

"I might suggest that *I'm* in charge, Walter," she said

coolly. "But it seems to me, right now, whoever's in control of Air Force One is in charge."

Dean took that in with a frown, as Colonel Michael Lange, United States Marines, entered the Situation Room with a black briefcase handcuffed to his wrist. Lange saluted the Vice-President, who returned his salute, as he proudly displayed the new nuclear football.

"Madame Vice-President," the marine said, "Mr. Secretary . . . All compromised nuclear launch codes have been canceled. New codes are active."

Sighs and smiles of relief were exchanged around the table as the Vice-President said, "Thank you, Colonel," and the marine took a seat.

General Northwood was just getting off the phone. He turned his doleful gaze on the Vice-President. "You and Walter may be right about Kazakhstan—the Moscow police report six members of a Russian TV news crew were found murdered on a roadside."

Bennett narrowed her eyes. "What connection does that have to our crisis?"

Northwood's expression was one of quiet disgust. "That news crew, from the program *600 Seconds,* was cleared to fly on Air Force One."

Bennett and Dean exchanged sharp, troubled glances, and both said, almost simultaneously, "What?"

"Looks like somebody took their place," Lee said.

"Six Russian males representing themselves as the *600 Seconds* crew are aboard Air Force One," Northwood said, "right now."

"Dear God," Bennett said, shaking her head, "tell me it's not that easy!"

"It's not," Lee said. "You'd have to generate flawless fake ID . . . photo . . . fingerprints."

"Could be inside help from Moscow," Northwood suggested.

"Are you joking?" Bennett said. "We've never been tighter with Moscow."

Dean was thinking it through. "Old-guard, pro-Radek forces within Petrov's government could accomplish that . . . but even so, there's no way to smuggle weapons on board Air Force One. It's impossible."

"Unless," Lee said reluctantly, "*our* security was breached."

Bennett, hating the thought, asked, "If our computers were programmed with false clearance information, you mean?"

Lee sighed and nodded.

"It would explain how the terrorists got their weapons," Bennett said. "Nobody smuggled anything aboard—there are already enough weapons onboard AFO to take Panama. Consider all the security aboard—air force guards, Secret Service."

"You think someone on the plane helped them?" Dean asked. "One of our own people?"

Bennett lifted an eyebrow. "Well, if so, that person, that traitor, is still up there, on Air Force One. That person may well be sitting among the hostages, gathering information. Who do they trust, up there? And if lines of communication open up—who can we trust?"

At another conference table—the one in the conference room of Air Force One, deep in the nighttime sky half a world away—hostages sat gathered around, while others hugged the walls, and the wounded were tended by the President's physician and air-force security guards whose training qualified them as medics.

Grace Marshall and her daughter, Alice, were huddled in one corner of the room, with Secret Service Agent Gibbs and her husband's two trusted advisers, Lloyd Shepherd and Jack Doherty, standing in front, shielding them. Grace's arm was around Alice, who clung to her mother, having reverted to a childlike state. The room was fairly quiet, with only occasional moans or sobs.

They were under the watchful eye of one of their armed captors, who trained his machine-gun pistol on them as he kept his position by the door, through which burst the leader—his name, Melanie Mitchell had told them, was Korshunov—followed by three more weapon-wielding terrorists.

Korshunov stood before the group, hands at his hips, as if he were going to break into a traditional Russian dance, except for the bulky weapon in one of those hands. He was disarmingly attractive, his features almost boyish; but his voice was harsh as he demanded, "Where is the wife? Where is the daughter?"

Grace entrusted Alice to Doherty as she pushed through Gibbs and Shepherd, and stood facing the captor. She was doing her best not to betray her fear and her voice was clear and did not quaver as she answered the terrorist's question with her own: "Where is my husband?"

Korshunov at first scowled, but his expression turned to one of apparent admiration.

"You are a brave woman. There is a power, even a dignity, in you that your husband, I'm afraid, sorely lacks."

She sneered at him. "What do you mean?"

There was a maniac twinkle in the smiling terrorist's eyes. "I mean, the coward has fled. He chose to save himself."

The escape pod, she thought. *Thank God!*

"But with you here," Korshunov said, and he looked over the heads of Gibbs, Shepherd, and the others, where they blocked Alice, "and your lovely daughter . . . Well, in my country, one can always find a way to strike a bargain."

She smiled at him, as cold and awful a smile as she could muster. "I don't know who you are or what you want, but I can tell you one thing: you'll never get it. The President of the United States will not negotiate with a terrorist like you."

"Really? I wasn't thinking of the President of the United States so much as I was of a husband . . . a father . . . who could not live with himself, if he were responsible for the deaths of his wife and daughter. Besides, it would be such bad public relations . . . bad politics. . . ."

Korshunov placed the snout of the machine-gun pistol to her head; it felt cold, and metallic, and rough. She swallowed, but held her ground.

"I think he'll negotiate," Korshunov whispered smugly, and he lowered the gun, patted her cheek gently, and exited through the line of his men, who backed out behind him, keeping their weapons trained on the hostages till they were out and the door slammed shut.

Alice pushed through the human barrier to go to her mother's arms, and hug her, and they comforted each other, but they did not cry. They were happy.

Grace's husband, Alice's father, was safe.

* * *

Vice-President Kathryn Bennett was on her feet, in the Situation Room, studying a map of Air Force One's trajectory displayed on one of the chamber's many wall screens: Moscow to Berlin and back toward the Black Sea.

"Madame Vice-President . . ."

She turned and it was young Peters, the communications officer, his expression wide-eyed.

"I have Air Force One," the communications officer said. "A man who refuses to identify himself wants to speak to you."

"Put me on room speaker," she said, and he nodded, went to his console, hit a button, nodding to her, mouthing, "We're on."

"This is the Vice-President of the United States," Bennett said, looking at the ceiling. "To whom am I speaking?"

A slightly hissy, staticky voice responded on the room's overhead speakers: *"This is the person who controls Air Force One. Perhaps you'll recall Air Force One—the world's most secure aircraft?"*

"What is it you want?"

"We'll get to that."

"Let me speak with the First Lady."

"No."

"I need to know she and her daughter are safe."

"You know the President is safe, do you not? You certainly know that he ran out of here like a whipped dog. I'm sure you are anxious for his return, so he can start making the decisions . . . so you can stop sweating through that silk blouse of yours. You are wearing a silk blouse?"

Bennett realized, suddenly, that she was on one end of the most momentous obscene phone call in history.

"Never mind what I'm wearing," she said. "What is the condition of the people onboard?"

"They're fine. Those who are not dead."

Around the Situation Room, expressions were solemn. Bennett looked at Dean, who was shaking his head in contempt, his mouth twitching into a grimace.

"What are your intentions?" she asked.

"What arrogance . . . to think you could ever understand my intentions."

"I need to understand what it is you want. Otherwise, how do you expect us to negotiate?"

"Then I will tell you what I want. I want Mother Russia to be a great nation again. I want to see the capitalists dragged from the Kremlin and into the streets and shot. I want to see our enemies cower at the mention of our name. I want to see America beg for our forgiveness, and on that great day of deliverance, you will understand, you will not need to ask, what it is that I want."

Bennett looked around the room and the faces confirmed her suspicion: they were dealing with a madman whose own life meant nothing to him. This was not a criminal who wanted money and a plane ride to Cuba. This was a man with a glorious cause.

"We can provide you with a forum for your grievances," Bennett said calmly. "We will contact the Russian government on your behalf, but these things take time. . . ."

"Well, then feel free to take your time. There is no rush . . . though you may wish to inform your cowardly president, when he's fished from his pod, this captain who deserted his ship, that we are holding his wife, his daughter, his chief of staff, his national security adviser, and,

what else? Oh yes, his baseball glove, which we found in his office. If he wants any of those items back, he might wish to prevail upon his puppet regime in Moscow to release the patriot, General Ivan Stravanovitch Radek. We will trade our fifty hostages and one baseball glove for one patriot. That's quite a bargain. And my dear, how is your blouse? Perspiration stains are a bastard to get out, aren't they?"

She *was* sweating, goddamnit; but her blouse wasn't silk.

"What assurance do I have," Bennett said coolly, "that you will keep your word?"

"How can I best demonstrate that I am a man of my word? Ah! Here's a way. . . . I will wait for confirmation that General Radek has been released. You will have half an hour—"

"Half an hour!"

"—at the end of which time, we will execute a hostage."

"No . . ."

"And on every half hour we wait beyond that time, we will execute another. You have my word."

And the click from the room speaker told everyone in the Situation Room that the line had gone dead.

An awful moment of silence followed, broken by General Northwood's outburst: "Goddamnit, nobody does this to the United States! The President will get his goddamn baseball glove back, all right, and use that bastard's balls for catch!"

"That's a valuable insight, General," Dean said.

"We can't negotiate General Radek's release in half an hour," Bennett said, pacing. "We need more time."

"It's tough negotiating with zealots," Lee observed. "All you can do is try to wear them down. . . ."

Bennett studied the glowing map. "And if we can't?"

"Mr. Secretary," said Communications Officer Peters, who had just gotten off the phone, handing a note to Dean.

As he read the note, the blood drained from Dean's face and he raised the back of his hand to his forehead, as if checking himself for a fever.

Then, his normally hooded eyes very wide, Dean said, "The pod has been located in the countryside outside Ramstein. . . . It's empty."

"Empty?" Northwood said, as if it were an exotic foreign word he couldn't fathom.

The rest of the room had fallen into a shocked silence, which was broken by Bennett's question: "Then where the hell is Jim Marshall?"

Dean's expression was grave. "I think we have to acknowledge the possibility that the President may be a casualty."

"He's too valuable a hostage to murder," Northwood snapped.

"He's also not the hostage type," Dean said.

"What do you mean?" Bennett asked.

With patience that was really condescension, Dean explained, "I mean, a Medal of Honor winner like James Marshall does not go down without a fight."

Kathryn Bennett knew that all too well. Jim Marshall was possibly the only candidate in either party who, at this point in history, could have won a presidential election with a female running mate. Marshall had been the Democrats' worst nightmare: a moderate-Republican version of Bill Clinton, minus the womanizing reputation, without a hint of personal or professional scandal, and a Vietnam veteran . . . a certified war hero . . . to boot.

"But if the President was killed in the takeover of the plane," Lee was saying, "why wouldn't their leader have told us?"

"To buy some time," Dean said. "To keep us negotiating, instead of retaliating."

"We'd retaliate all right," Northwood said. "We'd release General Radek . . . into the goddamn atmosphere."

"No, no," Bennett said, "this doesn't add up. That terrorist knew we'd recover the pod in short order. It was clear he expected us to take his demands to the President."

"Maybe we're burying Jim Marshall prematurely," General Greely offered, a tiny smile forming. "This is a man who flew more helicopter rescue missions than anyone else under my command. This is a man who knows how to fight."

"A soldier," Northwood agreed.

"Well, let's not start saluting the flag and playing John Philip Sousa," Bennett said. "If the President released that pod himself . . . and then secreted himself aboard Air Force One . . . he's taking an incredible chance with his life."

Greely said, "If so, it's the best chance we have."

Northwood said, "The element of surprise is a formidable advantage in combat."

"Oh, really?" Bennett returned, irritation rising in her like steam. "Well, that pod was designed for a reason, General. That pod was meant to protect your commander in chief, who has no right to risk his life."

"His family's on that plane," Northwood said.

"His 'family' is the American people. And his responsibility is to them." She drew in a deep breath. "I pray he's alive, but if he's entertaining thoughts of playing Rambo . . ."

"He's a shoo-in for the next election, if he pulls it off," Dean said wryly. "Not to mention the history books."

"Or perhaps he's just history," Bennett put in flatly.

Then she moved back to the conference table.

"Where's our backup Air Force One pilot?" she asked, sitting down. "And let's get a tape of that terrorist's dirty phone call for our behavioral-science people from FBI and CIA to have a go at it . . . ."

Around her, the advisers—military and civilian—took their chairs, as Kathryn Bennett gave orders and asked questions, while Walter Dean leaned back, a hand poised thoughtfully at his jaw, finger looped over his mouth, studying her with the cool appraising eye of a coach watching the opposing team in action.

*Chapter Ten*_____

Reasonably certain he was alone now, in the recesses of Air Force One's baggage deck, President James Marshall lowered himself from the overhead wing strut where he had tucked himself away, after sending the empty escape pod on its diversionary mission. His face was smudged—grease from somewhere—and he was mussed, a cowlick rising from his perfectly moussed presidential hair. One of the rolled-up sleeves of his white shirt had come loose, and he rolled it back up; the spatters of blood on the shirt were not his own: they belonged to Walters, the dead Secret Service agent on the gangway.

Marshall crouched over the body of the agent who had given his life to shield the President. The agent's coat was flipped open, revealing the empty holster; the body had been stripped of weapons. Walters stared into nothing, eyes as empty as a doll's. Saying a silent prayer, Marshall passed his hand over the agent's face, gently closing the unseeing eyes.

It had been many years since Jim Marshall had viewed the body of a man killed by gunfire; but the smell of cordite, and of bloody death, was all too familiar to the

Vietnam veteran. More than the sight of Walters, this smell brought home to Marshall the reality of his situation: war. This was war. And, above him, his family and many trusted friends and coworkers were prisoners of war.

He, however, was still a free agent. And the enemy soldiers who held this plane were relatively small in number; he would guess five, or maybe six. Those odds weren't insurmountable. He could pick them off one at a time, from the shadows.

But he had no weapon; the closest thing he had was his necktie, which could serve as a makeshift garrote. He shook his head, allowed himself a wry smile; he had gone from a James Bond villain's escape pod to thinking he *was* James Bond. Marshall . . . James Marshall.

Christ. After all these years, could he still fight, could he still kill? When he was twenty-two years old, he'd been part of a SpecOps team on a mission to destroy a Viet Cong munitions dump; but before the mission had really even begun, the copter had been shot from the sky, and only he had walked away from the wreckage. Bloody, half-dead, he had lived in the jungle and picked off VC one at a time before he finally blew that goddamn dump to hell and gone. He was in pretty bad shape when he stumbled out of that jungle, but stumble out he had. That's what had won him the Medal of Honor and, truth be told, probably the presidency.

But that had been a different Jim Marshall, a young Jim Marshall, a Jim Marshall trained in the ways of war. Not fifty-year-old President James Marshall who kept fit by jogging, when he could find the time. . . .

And even if he were up to the job, even if he could

wage one-man guerrilla war against these terrorists, he had the hostages to consider . . . his family among them.

If Grace and Alice were still alive (and they had to be alive, the terrorists would keep them alive as bargaining chips, he believed that, he *had* to believe that), they would be in increased danger, if the terrorists learned of Marshall's presence on the ship. The bastards could use Grace and Alice to draw him from hiding; or, should they capture Marshall, his family's value to the terrorists would decrease. There were a thousand ways these sons-of-bitches could use Grace and Alice against him. . . .

He had to conceal his presence; and he had to keep the hostages out of harm's way, avoid putting them in any cross fire.

Rather than head back to the front galley and the stairs up to the fore of the ship, he worked his way aft, padding along the gangway into the belly of the plane, pushing through the eerie shadows through a world of conduits and cable and jumbled angular pieces of machinery, a germ exploring a much larger creature's system. Perhaps he could find a weapon; perhaps some entry to the rear of the upper deck. . . .

He almost ran into one of the terrorists, a big man with (thank God!) his back to Marshall, and ducked into the shadows, tucking himself behind a strut. The terrorist turned around—he had a hawkish countenance—and fanned his machine-gun pistol around as he searched the darkness, then moved on.

Quietly, Marshall retreated, moving fore.

In the conference room, the hostages were now unattended, forty-seven men and women locked within a space designed to accommodate perhaps a dozen, at most. Claustrophobia and anxiety hung in the room like dark clouds flashing occasional lightning. They had been forced to hear the nightmarish conversation between Korshunov and Vice-President Bennett; the terrorist had piped it in from the Mission Communications Center over the intercom. Every half hour, the egomaniacal terrorist had said, one of them would be executed.

Huddled in the corner, cradling her daughter, Grace Marshall quietly listened to her husband's most trusted advisers, sitting like kids on the floor, bickering.

Jack Doherty, national security adviser, almost whined as he said, "How the hell did the bastards get on Air Force One in the first place, is what *I* wanna know!"

Deputy Press Secretary Melanie Mitchell, her mascara running, sat hugging her legs, looking like a homesick girl sitting around a campfire. "That was my fault. I invited them."

"You're goddamn right you did," Doherty spat. "If you weren't so concerned with getting the President on the MTV news, and keeping his quotient up with the 'Rock the Vote' crowd—"

"That's not fair," Chief of Staff Lloyd Shepherd said, and he placed a hand on Melanie's arm. "The President was in favor of bringing *600 Seconds* aboard; he did that with his eyes wide open."

Doherty's mouth remained tight with anger. "If she hadn't—"

"Security isn't her responsibility," Gibbs interrupted. The Secret Service agent gestured to himself, ruefully. "If you're going to blame anybody, blame me. You don't think our hosts are *really* from a Russian TV show, do you?"

"Hardly," Shepherd said. "The real crew's probably dead in a ditch somewhere."

Grace shuddered, held her daughter close.

"Well," Gibbs said, "I can guarantee you that when this is all over, there will be a full accounting of what took place, and what went wrong."

"I'm sure." Doherty smirked humorlessly. "Do the words 'Warren Commission' ring a bell?"

Major Caldwell, standing nearby, arms folded, back to the wall, suddenly joined in on the conversation. Crisply military, he said, "Blame and recrimination aren't going to get us off this plane. It's counterproductive."

Doherty sneered. "Fifty body bags and a fucking fork-lift are going to get us off this plane."

Melanie Mitchell began to weep and Alice clutched her mother, who snapped at Doherty, "Stop it! Will you *stop* it!"

Doherty blinked at the First Lady's scolding, embarrassed.

"If Jim got off this plane alive," she said, "I'm sure he's doing everything in his power to solve this problem . . . and I think we should be doing the same."

Caldwell leaned in and whispered. "Gentlemen. It's a bit of a long shot, but if we could find a way out of this room, I think we might also be able to get off this plane. Air Force One is—"

"Major," Shepherd said, "this room is not secure."

Caldwell looked shocked. "This room is soundproof. Completely shielded . . ."

"No, he's right, Major," Doherty said. "Those 'newsmen' did not get aboard this plane without somebody's help . . . very possibly, somebody in this room."

And the little group discussion ended, as Grace Marshall looked from one face to another of her husband's most trusted confidants, wondering if one of them might be a traitor. The others were doing the same thing.

Except the Traitor, of course.

Moving through the lower forward galley as quietly as his presidential Florsheims would allow, Marshall made for the winding metal staircase and ascended, relieved to find the floor panel was still shoved aside. He edged up, gingerly, still standing on the stairs, most of him remaining in the stairwell as he checked to see if a guard had been posted.

But there was no guard.

Still poised mostly in the stairwell, peeking out of the hole like a cautious turtle from its shell, Marshall could get a view—in and around the circular metal stairway to the upper deck— down the hallway, where a tall, dark, pockmarked terrorist paced outside the conference room, machine-gun pistol cradled in his hands.

Ducking back down instinctively, as if he'd touched a hot stove, Marshall poked his head up again and slowly peered out. *They must be holding the hostages in the conference room,* he thought, and heard stirrings below him.

Footsteps.

Someone was moving through the galley—toward the steps.

Cornered, Marshall popped out of his hole and dashed into the hallway, clunking footsteps on the metal stairwell

behind him, the sight of the terrorist posted at the conference room ahead of him . . . thank God the bastard's back
was to him!

And the President of the United States, hopping over
the dead Secret Service agent just outside the door, slipped
into his stateroom.

The guard in the hall, Krasin, heard something, but
when he turned only saw Nevsky, emerging from the
lower deck.

"All clear," Nevsky said.

Krasin nodded, as Nevsky headed up the circular stairs
to the Mission Communications Center.

In Washington, D.C., dusk was settling in. In the
Situation Room in the West Wing of the White House,
Vice-President Kathryn Bennett had long since settled
in, herself, in the chair at the head of the conference
table. On her left was Secretary of Defense Walter
Dean; on her right, Deputy National Security Adviser
Tom Lee, who was briefing the Vice-President from
some notes.

"What do the psyche profiles indicate?" she asked.
"How far do our experts estimate this madman will go?"

"Well, they agree that he *is* a madman," Lee said. "But
a controlled one. Delusional, not psychotic."

She frowned. "Meaning what?"

Lee sighed glumly. "Meaning he'll see this thing
through to the last hostage . . . or his own death."

"He's a Radek loyalist," Dean said, leaning back in
his chair, arms folded. "That tells us all we need to
know."

"Then if we do as he says," Bennett said, "and secure Radek's release—"

"Release that bastard," Dean said, sitting up, eyes flaring, "and all of Central Asia goes up in flames!"

Wearily, she said, "I understand the consequences, Walter."

"Do you?" Dean pushed back his chair and began to pace; he gestured toward the looming, glowing screens. "Such as, the return of the Soviet empire under a banner of genocide? A Russian Hitler like Radek bullying the world with a nuclear arsenal?" He stopped near Bennett's chair. Quietly he said, "It gives me no pleasure to say it, Kathryn, but fifty people is a small price to pay to prevent that."

She gazed at him unblinkingly. "Even if one of them is the President?"

He scowled, pawed the air. "The presidency is bigger than any one man . . . or woman. Didn't they teach you that at Yale?"

"Suppose," she said, over the tent of the fingers of both hands, "we release Radek today . . . secure the release of our hostages . . . and pick up the pieces tomorrow. We took Radek before, we can take him again."

"You may go to 'take him' again and find he's in Moscow," Dean said. "If Petrov releases Radek, I promise you Russia will fall. Radek won't be some international criminal, some petty dictator—he'll *be* the Russian government."

"With all due respect, Mr. Secretary," Lee said, in a tone that seemed refreshingly reasonable to Bennett, "we don't need melodrama, we need options—feasible options."

"Releasing Radek is *not* an option," Dean said, and took his seat.

Lee looked toward Bennett. "We need a decision, Madame Vice-President."

"It's not hers to make," Dean said, matter-of-factly.

"Oh?" Bennett asked. She and the deputy national security adviser were looking toward Dean as if he'd belched.

Dean's smile was faint, his eyelids at half-mast, as he leaned back in his chair, quietly cocky. "This is a military situation. I'm the secretary of defense. Check your regs. In the absence of the President, who to the best of our knowledge is still alive, I am next in the military chain of command."

And for a few moments, the only sound was that of Teletype machines spitting out paper.

"Tom," Bennett said evenly, "get the attorney general in here with a copy of the Constitution. . . . In the meantime, we have nineteen minutes before that madman kills his first hostage . . . and I'm going to consult with President Petrov."

Marshall found himself in the shambles of his stateroom.

Looking around the room—furniture overturned, bulletholes in the wood, puckers of bullets in other surfaces—he felt his stomach sink and his heart speed. His eyes searched the floor, the walls, for signs of carnage, but there were no telltale splashes or smears of blood. No signs, thank God, despite the obvious aftermath of gunfire, that his family had been slaughtered here in their little living quarters . . .

Cautiously, he moved through the bathroom into his

office, where it was if nothing had happened; nothing seemed disturbed—even the videotape of the Notre Dame game was still playing, the low chatter of sports announcers a reminder of another, more normal life. Crossing to his desk to try the intercom phone, he noticed his autographed World Series baseball glove was missing. What was *that* about?

The phone was dead.

Over the thrum of the 747 engines, he could hear a different, high-pitched engine hum; another plane? He went to a window and saw an F-15 flying close by. Beyond the F-15, another, and another. He tried to signal the closest one, but the pilot's attention was on the sky straight ahead.

Sounds from the hallway alerted Marshall, and as his office door began to open, he quickly ducked into the bathroom, and on through into the stateroom, tucking his back to the wall by the bathroom door. A bathroom mirror gave Marshall a view of the tall, pockmarked terrorist hallway guard entering the office, frowning, eyes narrowed, attention perked as if he'd heard something in the office and was checking it out.

Which meant the hallway should be clear now, and the conference room unguarded, momentarily at least, and Marshall exited the stateroom just as a click and the abrupt absence of sports-announcer chatter signaled the TV being turned off by the terrorist.

In the hallway, the President made his way toward the conference room, and the hostages, *they* must *be in there,* when a beeping startled him. Knowing the noise would alert the guard, Marshall ducked inside the nearest cabin. . . .

Drawn by the beeping, Vladimir Krasin stepped out of the presidential office into the hallway, which he found empty, though the noise continued. Krasin moved toward the sound, stopping at the dead Secret Service agent who had fallen outside the stateroom.

The noise was emanating from the agent's wrist—his watch; an alarm was going off, a reminder for a dead man of something that had no doubt lost its importance.

Krasin moved past the corpse, on his way to resume his guard position by the conference room, when he noticed that the door to the staff cabin was ajar. This was a room Krasin himself had checked out earlier, and he seemed to remember shutting that door tight, making sure it was secure. . . .

Staying poised in the doorway, Krasin eyeballed the darkened room, which had tables and desk chairs and some overhead cabinets; this was not as elaborate an office as the one the marine colonel had been shot in, at the paper shredder. It seemed to be a staff cabin, and the cabinets (which Krasin had earlier checked out) contained, among other things, medical supplies.

Nothing suspicious here.

But then Krasin considered a certain tall cabinet, a freestanding closet the staffers used to hang coats; and it occurred to him that a man might be able to hide in there. He stepped into the room to check it out, reaching with his free hand for the light switch when something gripped his neck and pulled him back.

Stepping from where he'd been tucked behind the door, Marshall yanked with his double-hand grip on the necktie he had looped around the terrorist's neck, but

Krasin elbowed him in the solar plexus, and Marshall loosed his grip as he doubled over in pain. The terrorist, reaching behind him, flipped Marshall, sending him careening across the room, slamming into a desk chair, sending it spinning into Krasin's path, buying Marshall enough time to get to his feet and leap at the terrorist, even as Krasin was bringing his gun up to shoot. Marshall drove Krasin into a corner of the room, slamming the man's head into the wall.

But Krasin was a much younger man than Marshall, who was up against a physical specimen who could have matched the young Marshall of Vietnam days, and the terrorist quickly recovered, and responded, grabbing Marshall by the shirtfront, shoving him into the opposite wall, and the force of Marshall's back slamming into the wall accidentally turned on a light switch.

And in a room flooded with light, Vladimir Krasin, poised to shoot with his machine-gun pistol, suddenly knew who his opponent was: the President of the United States.

And in that frozen moment, his open eyes and dropped-open mouth indicating the difficulty Krasin was having processing this information, a moment Krasin might have better spent firing his MP-5, Marshall dove into the terrorist in a tackle worthy of Notre Dame.

Krasin was on his back, but he hadn't fumbled the weapon, and as Marshall clawed for it, tried to pry it from the Russian's fingers, Krasin held fast, and bucked, shoving his forearm up into Marshall, who kept his left hand pressed down on the weapon in Krasin's right, drawing back enough to send a hard right cross into Krasin's jaw.

But the terrorist still clung to the gun.

Rolling, twisting, clinging like lovers, they struggled for the damn thing, nearing the door, and Marshall squeezed both hands around Krasin's wrist, the MP-5 suddenly popping from the man's grasp, flying out the open door, clunking to the carpeted hallway.

Marshall dove off the Russian and scrambled out the door, scooping up the weapon, but Krasin pounced right on top of him, pulling him like a big fish into a boat, back into the room.

Then it was the Russian diving for the gun, but he never made it out the door, Marshall grabbing onto him, hurling him to the floor, kicking him in the solar plexus. But, damn, the Russian was getting up again, a fucking zombie that couldn't be killed, and Marshall reached for the first thing, the only thing, within his reach, a small stool, which he smashed across Krasin's upper body, including his face, and the terrorist went down and, finally, stayed down.

His breath heaving, Marshall stumbled into the hallway, scooped up the weapon, then knelt at the unconscious Russian and took a ring of keys from the man's belt. Then he rushed to the door of the conference room, where he tried a key.

Wrong one.

He tried another, and another. . . .

A bullet slammed into the wooden door, and Marshall whirled, but the MP-5 was drooping at his side.

The terrorist, his face bloody, looking only about half-conscious, stood there with a small handgun, an automatic, pointed right at Marshall.

Should have searched the son-of-a-bitch, Marshall thought, and wondered why the Russian hadn't shot to kill.

"Drop the gun," the terrorist said, his accent thick as sour cream on borscht. "I don't want to kill so valuable a hostage."

That answered Marshall's question, and it was also the exact wrong thing for Krasin to say.

The President of the United States swung the MP-5 up and opened fire.

The bullets slammed into Krasin, the assault vest stopping some of them, but not the force of their impact, though the rounds that hit above the vest, one in his neck, another in his right cheek, and one in the forehead, just under a scar he'd had since he was a boy when he fell from a tree, killed Krasin right now. His brain was a blank screen before his body had even tumbled to the hallway carpet.

James Marshall, though stunned by what he'd done, had little time for contemplation of his act; he knew the gunfire would alert the other terrorists, who he supposed were in the fore of the plane, in the Mission Communications Center and on the flight deck.

So he did what any brave, smart soldier would do: he retreated.

He ran down the corridor, toward the aft of the plane, glimpsing through open doors the corpses of Colonel Perkins in its shower of shredded paper (and Marshall immediately knew what this courageous man had accomplished) and in the Secret Service cabin, the three dead agents leaned back in their first-class seats, while behind him terrorists came rattling down the metal winding stair-way from the upper deck.

On the run, he fired the MP-5 back at them, and they sought cover while he pressed on. Soon he was at the end of the line, moving through the rear press cabin, rounding the corner of the rear galley, facing the three rest rooms, their doors open, flapping, applauding his empty efforts.

With no idea that it was the President they were chasing, thinking a stray Secret Service agent was on the loose, Lenski and Nevsky were the first to reach the rear of the plane, but Marshall was nowhere to be seen. They exchanged glances, in agreement that their prey must surely be behind one of the three closed rest-room doors.

Nevsky fired an MP-5 burst into the first rest-room door.

Then he repeated the process with the second door, and the third.

But when they opened the doors, in reverse sequence—third, second, first—the freedom fighters found them unoccupied.

And in the lower-deck rear galley, James Marshall was tumbling out of the cramped dumbwaiter that had been the only escape pod he'd used today, thank you. He brushed himself off, pulled himself together, and looked beyond the galley.

Baggage bins.

And he suddenly knew what to do.

He allowed himself a smile, as he began to search through the luggage, not opening any of them, but look-ing for a specific item, slinging aside garment bags and suitcases, until they littered the bulkhead.

Like a mouse seeking cheese deep in the bowels of some dark building, the President of the United States rummaged on.

*Chapter Eleven*_____

In the Situation Room at the White House, the buzz of activity halted as Vice-President Bennett spoke on the phone with President Petrov.

Unlike the call from the terrorist, this one was not piped in over the room speakers; this was a private call, although Bennett sat at the conference table surrounded by her advisers, Tom Lee again at her right hand, Walter Dean at her left. They, like their frozen underlings silhouetted against the looming high-tech screens around the room, were hanging on every word, extrapolating Petrov's side of the conversation from what they heard Bennett saying—and not saying.

The call was not going well. They were long past the apologies for waking the Russian president in the middle of a Moscow night; and were well beyond Petrov's sincere expressions of concern for the welfare of the President, his family, and the hostages on AFO. They were, in fact, going over the same frustrating ground, regarding the release of General Radek, for a third time.

"In eleven minutes, sir," Bennett said, "a hostage will be executed."

"Madame Vice-President," Petrov said wearily, his tone sad yet firm, "I cannot release this man."

"We would train all of our military might on this one target. I assure you, he would not stay at large for long."

"Perhaps." Petrov's voice was so clear he might have been using a phone down the street. "But seizing a man like Radek *once* is a feat of military genius. Doing so a second time, in the face of renewed security, is a miracle."

"There are those who would say that an alliance between our two countries is a miracle, President Petrov. . . ."

"And there are those who call it an abomination. Madame Vice-President, you are trying to save a handful of hostages. I am trying to save a nation."

"President James Marshall is on that plane, sir. You know better than anyone that no nation can easily survive, or soon replace the loss of a great leader."

Petrov's sigh held no impatience; only regret. "I consider James Marshall a friend, but also an ally in the war against the beast you would have me release. Let us be pragmatic, Madame Vice-President. Fifty lives means nothing in the grand scheme. Millions of lives hang in the balance, here. Do not let your emotions blind you."

Bennett twitched a frown at what she took to be a reference to her sex; then she responded coolly and firmly. "Then I will be equally pragmatic, President Petrov. I will remind you that our president took a great risk to come to your aid, against strong opposition in both parties and even among our allies."

There was a humanity in Petrov's hushed voice that Bennett found moving, even as his words gave her hope: "If it meant saving his life, I would do it."

"James Marshall is aboard that plane, President Petrov."

"Yes . . . but is he alive? Have you had contact with him?"

"He has no way to contact us."

"You cannot tell me he is alive, can you?"

Now it was Bennett who sighed. "No. No, I cannot, Mr. President."

"Then I am sorry," he said. *"Dos vidania."*

"Dos vidania," she said, and the click of the phone hanging up, across the world, was like the cocking of a gun.

"Nine minutes," Lee said.

Bennett, staring into nothing, nodded and, without looking at her secretary of defense, said, "Walter, you and General Northwood and General Greely get your heads together. We've got to find a feasible option . . . and fast."

"Yes, ma'am." Dean was taking no pleasure in this; his expression was somber. "But you need to know . . ."

"Yes?"

"We're going to lose at least one hostage. That man was not bluffing."

"No he wasn't." And she gave him a smile that had little to do with smiling. "I would say skyjacking Air Force One was the act of man not inclined to make empty threats."

And Dean was up and out of the room, and the room was bustling back to life, even as Kathryn Bennett leaned forward, cupping her face in one hand, closing her eyes, wondering why she had ever wanted this responsibility.

In another, if less expansive high-tech room of screens and blinking lights—the Mission Communications Center

on the upper deck of Air Force One—Ivan Korshunov
paced like an angry cat.

"I don't want him in the same room with *them*," Korshunov was saying in Russian to Igor Nevsky and Boris
Bazylev.

They were discussing the remains of the freedom fighter
Vlad Krasin—specifically, Korshunov's insistence that
his body not be stored with the corpses of the enemy
dead that had been piled in one cabin.

Nevsky said, "He rests in a cabin, alone."

Korshunov planted himself in front of the hawk-faced
freedom fighter. "Vlad does not rest, Igor. He rots. And
unless we find his murderer, he may soon have company
in his decay."

Sergei Lenski burst into the communications center,
having just rechecked the rear galley where Vlad's killer
had seemingly disappeared.

"He's on the lower deck," Lenski said, gesturing downward with a thumb. "He used a dumbwaiter to escape
us. . . . I jammed a drawer into the thing and disabled it."

"Go," Korshunov said to Bazylev, who nodded curtly
and rushed out, his footsteps on the metal stairs telling
the story of his quick pursuit of the intruder.

"Afghanistan," Korshunov muttered. "Five years at my
side and not a scratch, and now *this* . . ." He was pacing
again, slamming a fist into an open hand. "Who *is* this
murderer?"

"I checked the manifest," Nevsky said. "Everyone is
accounted for."

"Sergei, check the dead," Korshunov said. "Make sure
the Secret Service and air-force guards are truly dead.
Put an extra bullet in their heads."

Lenski nodded and went out.

Around the room various LED readouts gave the time: 3:29 A.M.

"Three minutes," Korshunov said, noting this. "Transfer the White House call to the conference-room phone."

And with a nod to Nevsky to follow him, Korshunov strode from the room. It was almost time to demonstrate his resolve, and repay in kind the butchering of a courageous freedom fighter.

In the Situation Room at the White House, Bennett sat listening to Walter Dean, whose expression was grim. Generals Northwood and Greely had again joined them at the conference table.

"Obviously, they can't keep that plane in the air indefinitely," the secretary of defense said.

"Obviously," the Vice-President said.

Dean gestured to one of the glowing wall-size maps. "There are only four potential refueling sites in Kazakhstan that are still controlled by Radek's forces. We have to go in and take them . . . simultaneously . . . in four surgical strikes."

Bennett frowned. "Can we do that?"

General Greely said, "I'd rather take my chances in the air."

With an impatient, dismissive wave, Dean said, "I've looked at your airborne scenarios, General. They don't cut it."

"Can we *do* this?" Bennett repeated.

"Yes," Northwood sighed, "but the casualty rate could surpass the number of hostages we're attempting to save."

"It's the military's job to risk its life in the defense of innocent civilians," Dean said with withering condescension.

"In three minutes," Bennett said, "they execute the first hostage."

"You're going to lose several hostages," Northwood said, shaking his head, "before we can put our ground scenario in motion. . . . Four coordinated strikes, four targets on foreign soil . . ."

"You're going to have to buy us some time, Kathryn," Dean said, and there was nothing patronizing in his tone.

"What kind of time?"

General Greely said, "It's four hours till they reach Kazakhstan airspace."

"Four hours," Bennett said. She closed her eyes. "Eight hostages."

And two minutes until the first would die.

"Place the call now," Bennett said to her communications officer, "and put it on the room speakers."

Nevsky unlocked the conference room door and opened it for Korshunov to go in. The room was deathly quiet, hostages seated at the big table and lining the walls, some seated, some standing, faces ashen with fear, eyes red with worry.

Korshunov, MP-5 in hand, crossed to the phone at the table; hostages scooted away on their chairs to make room, and he nodded and smiled his thanks to them for their thoughtfulness.

"I would like Mrs. Marshall and her lovely daughter to step forward," Korshunov announced.

A collective gasp rose from the hostages, torn as they

were with relief at not hearing their own names called for execution and dismay that the First Family should be so summoned. No one had expected this. In a game of chess, usually the pawns go first.

But Grace and Alice Marshall—behind the human wall provided them by National Security Adviser Doherty, Chief of Staff Shepherd, Secret Service Agent Gibbs, and Major Caldwell—did not respond to the order.

Korshunov, wearing a blandly affable expression, fired his machine pistol in their direction, over the heads of the hostages, some of whom screamed and dropped down, though the human wall of presidential insiders stayed intact before the First Family.

Then Grace gently told her protectors to let her by, and they reluctantly complied as she stepped forward with her daughter, an arm around the girl's shoulder.

"Mrs. Marshall," Korshunov said, gesturing with the machine pistol as if it were a cocktail in his hand, "Alice. Please understand I take no pleasure in this. Your government has put me in the unfortunate position of having to demonstrate my determination."

Doherty stepped forward from the wall of hostages. "Excuse me, sir."

Korshunov regarded Doherty's intrusion with mild amusement. "Yes?"

"I'm Jack Doherty, national security adviser."

"High-ranking," Korshunov said, as if impressed.

Doherty smiled mildly, reasonably. "You have the better part of the administration locked in this room. If you want to negotiate, we're the ones to do it with."

His voice alive with interest, Korshunov said, "Really?"

"At the White House, I'd be the one the President

would be listening to. Right now you're negotiating with the Vice-President."

Korshunov shrugged. "The President is not available. The coward has not yet returned to Washington."

"Unfortunately," Doherty said, "in our system of government, the Vice-President is just a figurehead . . . sort of like the Queen of England."

"I appreciate this, Mr. Doherty, this lesson in American political science."

Doherty took another step forward, gestured to the phone on the table in front of Korshunov. "If you'll just let me speak to the White House, I promise you, I'm the person who can best facilitate your—"

And the phone rang.

Korshunov raised a shushing finger for Doherty's benefit, and picked up the phone. Only Korshunov heard the Vice-President's words; he was not having the conversation piped in, this time.

"We need to explore our options," the Vice-President said in lieu of a greeting.

"Has General Radek been released?"

"I have contacted the Russian government," she said. "I am making arrangements with President Petrov, putting the wheels in motion—"

"Has General Radek been released?"

"Not at this point. We need to be realistic. It's going to take more time."

"You would like more time."

"Yes."

"I can give you another half an hour."

"That may not be enough."

"But it would be a start?"

"Yes."

Korshunov savored the relief he heard in the Vice-President's words.

"Good," Korshunov said. "We understand each other."

He placed the phone receiver on the table.

"Mr. Doherty," Korshunov said, "would you like to help me . . . what was your word? Facilitate my wishes?"

Doherty brightened. "Yes, sir."

"Very well," Korshunov said, and shot Doherty in the head.

The single round from the MP-5 was like a crack of thunder in the small room. Doherty, his eyes wide, his mouth open, the hole in the front of his head much smaller than the one in the back of his head, took a moment before falling, face-first, to the carpet, with a *whump,* to the accompaniment of hostages screaming.

The phone receiver on the table had sent these horrifying sounds to the Situation Room at the White House.

Korshunov picked up the phone and said, calmly, "Your national security adviser has just been executed. Pity for you to lose such an excellent negotiator. But he did buy you that half hour you wanted."

And he slammed the phone into the hook.

"Mrs. Marshall," Korshunov said politely, "Alice? If you would come with me, please . . ."

He held out his hand—the one not holding the machine pistol—and gestured to them as if he were inviting them out onto a ballroom dance floor.

Their eyes huge with fear, Grace and Alice Marshall accepted his invitation and stepped into the hall.

"Dispose of that garbage, would you?" he asked

Nevsky, who dragged the corpse of the national security adviser from the room, leaving a ghastly bloody trail.

Then the door closed quietly, leaving the hostages to contemplate the next half hour.

Or, actually, twenty-eight minutes. The clock had already begun to tick on the fate of some unlucky soul in this room.

In the baggage hold, piles of suitcases and garment bags littered the gangway like the floor of a ransacked room. And the President of the United States, his white shirt torn and bloody, his face smudged with dirt and bruises, was grinning like a burglar who had just come upon a valuable stash.

He had found Lloyd Shepherd's slim briefcase, which was not really a briefcase at all, but an Inmar-Sat portable phone. He had never used one of these things, so after he opened the attaché lid, activating the satellite unit, his first move was to flip through the instruction book. James Bond never had to do that.

He had hoped to find a list of phone numbers; Shep had all kinds of numbers loaded into the autodial, Marshall had seen him use the phone in that fashion countless times. But apparently those numbers seemed to be nowhere but in Shep's memory.

If he hadn't been consumed by so many other emotions, Marshall would have felt humiliated, realizing he—the President of the United States—did not know any of the vital, unlisted numbers at the White House.

Something Marshall had suspected from the beginning of his term had hit him headlong, here on this plane, in these dire circumstances: the President was too pampered, too protected, too isolated from real life. Everything was done for a president, even much of his thinking.

So he would have to call the White House's general number . . . only, what was it? He had never dialed it in his life.

And in the hold of Air Force One, held by terrorists, his shirt red with his own blood and that of an enemy he'd killed, his wife and daughter the hostages of homicidal zealots, the President of the United States dialed information, seeking the number of the house where he lived.

They charged him fifty cents for the call.

A gracious host, Korshunov provided seats for Grace and Alice Marshall in the high-tech surroundings of the Mission Communications Center on the upper deck.

Korshunov knelt by the seated girl. "This is the first time you have seen a man killed, hah?"

Alice said nothing. Her jaw was tight, crinkly, but she did not seem near tears. She was a brave girl.

"Leave her alone," her mother said.

He admired the First Lady's courage, as well; she was a better, stronger person than her cowardly husband.

Still kneeling before the child, Korshunov was gentle as he said, "You think I'm a monster, killing this man. He was someone's son. Someone's father, most likely."

"He had two children," Grace Marshall said.

His attention on the daughter, Korshunov said, "I have three children, and a wife I love very much. . . . Does that surprise you?"

The girl didn't reply; her eyes were cold.

"Tell her to answer," Korshunov said to the mother.

"Leave her alone, you sadistic son-of-a-bitch."

Korshunov rose, snarling, "Shut up!"

He had raised a hand to strike the First Lady, when the girl blurted, "Why did you kill Mr. Doherty?"

Lowering his hand, Korshunov, reasonable again, but not kneeling down, said to the girl, "Because I believe."

The girl's lip curled in contempt. "In what?"

"In Mother Russia. When I shoot a man, an enemy of my people, I know in that instant how deep my convictions run. Any doubts, any fears, any pang of conscience, these are swept aside by the depth of my belief. Do you understand, child?"

"No."

He twitched a tiny smile. "Well, understand this. To you, I'm a terrorist."

The girl's lip curled again. "To anybody you're a terrorist. I've seen the pictures from the refugee camps, kids my age with their arms hacked off by your soldiers."

Grace Marshall said, "Alice, please don't talk to him."

"Shut up," Korshunov snapped at the mother. Then to the daughter he said, "You are well-informed for one so young. Perhaps you would appreciate a lesson in current events."

"Not from you."

"Alice, don't," her mother said.

"A world leader," Korshunov began, his voice teacherly, "sends soldiers halfway around the globe to kidnap the president of a foreign land. This land is not at war with the invading country, has done nothing to provoke or prompt this lawless act. In the process, dozens of defending soldiers of the foreign land are butchered by the invaders, and their house of state, their White House, if you would, is destroyed by a bomb, and many civilian employees of the government are killed. What would you call such a world leader, such a man? I would call him a terrorist. And that is the lesson for this session: I am a freedom fighter, and your father is the terrorist."

Alice's chin trembled, but her eyes remained cold. "That's not true."

He gave out a single harsh laugh. "Why do you think you were vacationing in Moscow? To celebrate your father's great victory! To cheer this murderer and kidnapper and coward!"

"Stop it!" Grace said.

"Shut up!" Korshunov snarled.

"That's different," Alice said, "and you know it."

"Why, because your father is a terrorist in a suit and tie, who kills with a telephone call and a smart bomb?"

She lifted her chin, proudly. "You're a monster, and my father is a great man."

Korshunov raised his machine-gun pistol and pointed the ominous weapon at the child's head. "Perhaps it's time for another lesson."

"Please," Grace Marshall said. "She's just a child. She doesn't know what she's saying. . . ."

Korshunov lowered his gun. He studied the girl.

"You remind me of my middle daughter," he said, and he stroked the girl's hair and kissed her forehead.

"More lessons later," he said, and went through the blown-open hatchway onto the flight deck, settling into the copilot seat next to Kolchak.

*   *   *

In the baggage hold, James Marshall had just gotten the White House switchboard on the satellite phone.

"How may I direct your call?" The voice sounded chipper and very young.

"Okay, now," Marshall said, "listen carefully. This is an emergency call from Air Force One. Put me through to the Vice-President."

"You want to speak to the Vice-President," the switchboard operator said; the bored amusement in her voice dismayed Marshall.

"Yes, this is an emergency, and this is the President speaking."

"President of what?"

"Of the United States of America. Don't cut me off. I'm on Air Force One and this is an emergency."

"Look, whoever you are, get a life, before I trace this call and you find how wrong a number you've picked to make a crank call—"

"Trace the goddamn call! Follow standard security procedures and do it right now."

"If you want to make a federal case out of it," the switchboard operator said defensively, "it's fine by me. You're the one that will be talking to the FBI—"

"Don't move!"

Marshall looked behind him, and to the left.

The voice belonged to a blond, stocky terrorist who had Marshall cold; but did the bastard, advancing up the gangway, know what Marshall was doing there in the shadows? Had he heard Marshall talking? Had he seen, could he see, the phone? With Marshall's left side to the man, perhaps not . . .

The small phone receiver still to his ear, Marshall could hear that the line remained open; carefully, he slipped the small phone, with what he prayed was an open line to the White House, into his pocket, praying as well that the terrorist did not see what he was doing. . . .

"Give me the gun," the terrorist said, approaching, "very slowly."

Turning in slow motion, Marshall held out his weapon to the advancing terrorist.

And in his pocket, very muffled, so muffled even Marshall couldn't make it out, blessedly hidden by the thrum of the 747 engines, the voice of the switchboard operator— before whose eyes, back in Washington, was displayed a graphic digital display: TRACE CONFIRMED—WHITE HOUSE SAT ACCOUNT 33425—was saying, "Oh my God . . . Sir? Are you there? Hold on, I'll connect you. . . ."

Chapter
Twelve_____

In the Situation Room at the White House, Vice-President Bennett was on the phone briefing the secretary of state when Communications Officer Peters approached and waved at her with the manic anxiety of a child asking its teacher to leave the room.

"A moment, Mr. Secretary," Bennett said, covered the mouthpiece, and, with the barest nod, granted Peters permission to speak.

"Switchboard has a call from someone claiming to be the President," Peters said, words spilling out. "Traced the call to a White House satellite account . . . caller's gone but the line is still active."

"Something urgent, Mr. Secretary," Bennett said, hung up the phone, and to the communications officer ordered, "Put it through, on room speaker."

Peters nodded, went away, and quickly did that. The bustling room—minions at their workstations around the looming screens as well as the high-level advisers at the conference table—fell silent. Muffled voices, distorted, crackly, breaking up, came over the speakers; and so did the unmistakable whine of aircraft engines.

"Can we clean that up?" Bennett snapped.

At her left hand, Secretary of Defense Walter Dean picked up a phone, punched in numbers, and crisply said, "Max, get me Willis."

At the security listening post elsewhere in the West Wing, Willard Willis, a heavyset untidy man in his forties who was the White House's resident super-tech, worked at a console only slightly less complicated than a 747 instrument panel, pudgy fingers flying over a keyboard, wavelength images on monitors dancing as he implemented digital filtering.

"Hold on, Mr. Secretary," Willis said, "it's a damn weak signal. Tracking . . . intercepting . . . improving. Give me five more seconds, Mr. Secretary, and you could put this baby out on a CD."

And five seconds later a man's voice—perhaps not the CD quality promised, but clear as a call across town—filled the Situation Room, all eyes raised as if expecting to hear the voice of God.

"Listen to me . . . listen to me . . ."

An elated eruption of relief rocked the room at the sound of one of the most familiar, recognizable voices on the American scene.

"Do you know who I am? I am the President of the United States. . . ."

Dean's smile was a grimace as he pounded the conference table with his fist, once. "He's alive! Thank God."

"I know who are you," another male voice said, a thickly Russian-accented voice that no one in this room had ever heard before but, in a terrible way, every one of them immediately recognized. *"Put your hands above your head—move!"*

And the jubilation that had gripped them was replaced with deathly silence, as the Situation Room listened in on a deadly airborne confrontation, half a world away.

On the lower deck of the ship, the gangway littered with baggage, James Marshall stepped from the semi-darkness, hands in the air, satellite phone in his pocket. Before him stood a blond, stocky terrorist with a machine pistol, identical to the one Marshall had just handed over.

"Don't think I won't shoot you," the terrorist said, eyes wide, slinging Marshall's MP-5 on its strap over his shoulder. Expecting to find a Secret Service agent, the terrorist was obviously shocked to find he'd landed such a big fish.

"Don't do anything hasty," Marshall said. "I'm the one hostage you don't want to use up too quickly. I mean, this is your lucky day."

"Move," the terrorist said, gesturing with the machine pistol for Marshall to get in front of him, which Marshall did. "Keep those hands up!"

"Easy, take it easy," Marshall said, moving slowly down the gangway. "I mean, what can my people do now? Send in the F-15s to shoot the plane down? Even if they tried, Air Force One is equipped with tactical countermeasures."

"Why are you telling me this?" the terrorist asked, confused. "Why are you talking?"

"I just don't want you to do anything rash."

"Rash?"

Marshall stopped, hands still up, and glanced over his shoulder, giving his captor a resigned smile. "You know, impulsive . . . reckless . . . There's no need. You have me. You've won."

"I know we've won—keep moving!"

Marshall moved on—slowly. "You got nothing to worry about. The plane's computer would fly circles around any missile they shot at us." He paused again, threw another weary smile over his shoulder. "We wouldn't get hit, just a shock wave. . . ."

The terrorist, unsettled by Marshall's almost good-natured banter, whacked him in the back with the stock of the MP-5. "I said, keep moving!"

Marshall stumbled on. "Okay, okay . . . just believe me when I tell ya, if they fired on us, we'd get knocked on our butts, but that's all."

"Goddamnit, quit talking! Just move!"

And the President walked on, but took his time, hoping that phone line was still open, and the messages he'd sent had been received.

They had.

In the Situation Room, Bennett and Dean and several others, including the two generals, Greely and Northwood, had risen from their seats while the conversation between the President of the United States and the terrorist who held him played over the speakers like a radio drama. They had watched the ceiling, as if a visualization of the confrontation might appear there.

"My God," General Greely breathed, "is he asking us to do what I think he is?"

"He's told us what to do," Bennett said. "And we have to act now."

"It's too damn risky!" Dean said.

"Our president is up there with a gun at his back," Bennett said.

"Jesus Christ," General Northwood said, his eyes like Ping-Pong balls. "He's asking us to fire a goddamn missile at Air Force One!"

"And he's calculated the consequences," Bennett said coolly, and she turned a steady gaze on the secretary of defense. "Besides which, he's not asking. He's your commander in chief, and as far as I'm concerned, he just issued a direct order."

Dean's mouth flinched in a frown, but he nodded and went to the phone, saying, "Patch me through directly to Colonel Carlton."

In the cockpit of his F-15, Colonel Frank Carlton—Halo flight leader, in charge of the escort being given Air Force One—received a direct command from the secretary of defense.

It was a command he had never, under any circumstances, expected to hear.

"Sir, you're sure that's what you want me to do?"

And the voice of Walter Dean in Carlton's headset was as clear as the secretary's language. "You heard me, Colonel—but do not, I repeat do *not*, take your best shot."

"Roger," Carlton replied, and, shaking his head, he alerted his squadron to one hell of a situation: "Give some room, boys—I've been ordered to fire on Air Force One."

And the other five planes flared out, their bewildered pilots putting some distance between them and the 747 as Carlton's plane dropped back to position.

In his cockpit, Carlton said, "Missiles armed."

In moments, the image on his targeting computer was perfectly aligned.

"Target acquired," Carlton said, still not quite believing this. "I have a good lock."

His fingers hesitating over the flight stick, the Halo flight leader said, "God, I hope this works. . . . Fox Three."

He triggered the missile, and from under the Eagle the air-to-air missile detached, its tail igniting in flames, screaming through the sky, on its way to destroy Air Force One.

The big plane took a sudden, sharp, sloping dive, throwing everyone aboard AFO off balance, the hostages in the conference room, the terrorists in the Mission Communications Center—and their special hostages, the First Lady and her daughter—and the terrorist Boris Bazylev, who was walking his hostage, President James Marshall, along the lower-deck gangway.

The banking dive of the plane, however, did not give Marshall an opportunity to take the weapon away from the terrorist—Bazylev merely stumbled and recovered—and the President remained a captive.

But in the Mission Communications Center, Korshunov was yelling at his pilot, Kolchak, who had not been in the cockpit, the ship operating off autopilot.

"Get in there!" Korshunov shouted. "Do your job!"

But Kolchak had already scrambled through the blasted-open doorway to the flight deck, where he was climbing into the captain's seat, filling his hands with the double horns of the wheel, his eyes wide with the awful messages that had lighted up on the 747's instrument panel: MISSILE LOCKED . . . AUTOPILOT DISENGAGED . . .

And in the sky above and behind them, the comet-tailed heat-seeking missile was making a wide arc toward the banking plane.

Korshunov crawled into the copilot's seat, shouting, "What the hell is this? What the hell is going on?"

"The Americans fired on us," Kolchak said, astounded.

"What? On their own hostages! What kind of people are they? Bastards!"

A tactical digital display popped on: ACTIVATING COUNTERMEASURES.

Korshunov saw that and yelled, "What the hell does that mean?"

"I don't know!" Kolchak yelled back, his fingers clawing at controls. "We're fucked!"

A computer on the instrument panel was charting the missile closing in on the plane; another disconcerting message appeared in LED letters: MISSILE CLOSING . . . METALLIC DIVERSIONARY BURST STANDING BY . . .

Korshunov bellowed, "Do *something*!"

"I'm not a combat pilot!"

Now the monitor displayed the seconds to impact . . . *8 . . . 7 . . .*

And the missile screamed through the sky, trailing smoke and fire, as it bore in on the slow, easy target that was Air Force One.

. . . 5 . . . 4 . . .

The two Russians in the cockpit sweated and swore and perhaps made peace with a God they'd long ago abandoned as they watched the encroaching end of their lives on the TV of the computer display, charting the course of the missile about to impact their plane, even as small bay doors beneath the 747 yawned open, spraying a cloud of metallic particles out of the bottom of the aircraft.

Korshunov and Kolchak could not see the missile swerving off its course, onto a new, downward path; nor did they notice the computer's tactical display: MISSILE NEUTRALIZED.

But the missile indeed veered downward, diving into the swarm of descending metallic chaff and detonating, lighting up the night sky in a momentary dawn of red flames reflecting against silver-gray clouds.

Talking over the explosion, Colonel Carlton in his F-15 cockpit was saying, "Negative impact—missile deflected," while in the Situation Room on the other side of the world, a collective sigh of relief was breathed by Bennett, Dean, Lee, and the rest.

There was no time for celebration on Air Force One, which was immediately rocked by a shock wave: the Russians in the cockpit—who'd taken their seats so quickly they hadn't even buckled in—were tossed about the flight deck like rag dolls; the hostages were bounced around the conference room, suffering yet another indignity; while on the lower deck, the point of this exercise was about to be made.

James Marshall, waiting for this moment, grabbed and gripped the scaffolding and maintained his balance while the shock caught the terrorist off guard, making him totter like a top winding down. Marshall quickly turned and latched onto the terrorist's gun hand, slamming it into the steel wall until fingers popped open and the machine pistol fumbled to the floor with a clank.

Clutching the terrorist by his assault vest, Marshall whipped him around and smashed him into the metal wall, then flung him off the gangway and onto the pipes running under it.

Marshall was about to recover the dropped machine pistol when the terrorist—using the other machine pistol, the one taken from Marshall—let burst a rip of MP-5 rounds, Marshall diving out of the path of the gunfire, rolling into the forward galley.

The dimly lit galley provided shadows for Marshall to duck into, as he frantically looked around the little kitchen for some impromptu weapon.

But then the terrorist was moving into the galley, slowly, fanning the air with the MP-5, searching the near darkness for Marshall, who waited till the terrorist was turned away from him to move into the light with a right hand cocked for a roundhouse swing that damn near took the terrorist's jaw off, and did send the weapon flying from his hands, clattering to the floor.

This was another of these young tough Russians, however, and as before, Marshall soon had a fight on his hands that a man his age and in his only slightly above-average physical condition should not have to contend with. The hand that had held the weapon turned into a fist that crashed into Marshall's face, and then another fist was buried into his belly, so hard and deep it damn near touched his spine.

Spinning away, Marshall threw a wild punch out, which connected, tossing the terrorist backward, crashing him into and shattering the glass door of a refrigerator. The terrorist was caught there, half inside the refrigerator, and Marshall hauled him out, glass shards raining on the floor, tinkling like falling icicles, and threw a fist into the terrorist's face that knocked him back into a counter, stunning the man.

Like a wrestler applying a bear hug, Marshall grabbed the Russian from behind and squeezed the goddamn air out of his lungs and let him drop to the floor. Unconscious, apparently.

The President of the United States was breathing hard. He was exhausted and dazed by what he'd just been through. He stumbled over to the MP-5 and picked up the gun, catching his breath, wondering if he could survive this nightmare.

When he glanced around, the terrorist, a knifelike glass shard in one hand, was coming at him.

"Fuck you," Marshall breathed, and fired the weapon into the terrorist's face; his head exploded like a ripe melon and spattered the galley walls, the President's white shirt, and, to some degree, the President.

He stepped over the body, went to a sink, and washed the gore from a face that had been *Time*'s Man of the Year, not so long ago. He felt no remorse about what he'd just done; not a twinge of conscience, no pang of regret.

Jim Marshall was back in the jungle.

On the flight deck of Air Force One, Kolchak and Korshunov had found their way back into the seats. Kolchak had steadied the plane through the shock wave, and now all was calm. Relief and even joy filled the two men.

"Remarkable aircraft," Korshunov said. He called out into the Mission Communications Center. "Sergei! What's your situation?"

"Under control," Lenski called.

"Remarkable aircraft," Korshunov said again, smiling at the complexity of the instrument panel, the now calm computer monitors.

"Why did they do that?" Kolchak asked, still dumbfounded by the attack.

"Because they could," Korshunov replied. "To flex their muscles . . . but they made a stupid mistake."

"Yes?"

Korshunov's smile was also a sneer. "Now we know they cannot harm us, even if they wished to."

An excruciating tension had the Situation Room in its grip. They had heard the scuffle, the fight, over the phone line, piped over the speakers as if that radio show had taken a terrible turn—grunting, groaning, the unmistakable sounds of a vicious struggle, body blows, metallic clanking, glass breaking, and finally a gunshot!

The awful story these sounds had told was a muddy one. Who was the victor? What exactly had happened? For several long minutes, there was little more than silence—was that water running?—and, finally, the familiar voice came over the speakers.

"This is Marshall," the voice said.

And cheers went up around the Situation Room, then immediately quieted as the voice, strangely hard now, both weary and resolute, continued.

"Is anyone there?"

"We're here, Mr. President," Walter Dean said. "Where are you? What is your situation?"

"I'm on the lower deck of Air Force One. I've dispatched two terrorists . . . "

General Greely smiled, as if to say, I told you so.

". . . but I can only approximate the remaining number."

"We believe their number to be six," Dean said. "Or, four, now . . . They got aboard posing as those Russian newsmen."

"What do you know of my family? Are they safe? Alive?"

"The terrorists claim to be holding them," the Vice-President answered. "We can't confirm."

"Who the hell are they? What do they want?"

"They are Russian internationalist radicals," Dean said. "And what they want is the release of General Radek from prison."

"What are our tactical options?"

General Northwood took the ball. "They have us in a bad corner, Mr. President. We've ruled out a midair rescue; risks outweigh the potential results."

Greely pitched in: "Nothing we can do as long as the plane is in the air, sir."

"Ground action?"

"Under way," Northwood said. "We'll strike at the four Kazakhstan air bases under the control of Radek's regime in . . . three hours and forty-seven minutes."

"That's a long time, General. Bennett? Take me off that goddamn speakerphone. We need to talk."

The communications officer made that happen, and the

Vice-President lifted the phone receiver to her ear and said, "Yes, Mr. President?"

"We can't release Radek."

"They're going to shoot a hostage every half hour until we do," she said. "I don't want a plane filled with dead people."

"Do you think I do? My wife and daughter are on this plane."

"They've already shot Jack Doherty, Mr. President."

"Oh Christ."

"In full view of the other hostages."

"Bastards. Well, that doesn't change anything. We can't give in to their demands. There would be no end to it."

"And if you die on that plane, Jim? Will it end there?"

"No. Because you'll carry on, Kathryn. Whatever the cost. We have a job to do."

"Mr. President . . ."

"Kathryn, give a dictator an inch . . ."

She had heard him say this many a time; he was waiting for her to complete the sentence.

She did: ". . . and he'll invade Poland. Understood, Jim."

"Get this plane on the ground. Now I'm hanging up before the battery on this thing goes dead. Are we clear, Madame Vice-President?"

"Clear, Mr. President."

And the click in her ear told her the conversation was over.

"Well," Dean said to the Vice-President, keeping his condescension only partially in check, "I guess there's no argument about who's in charge now, is there?"

But Kathryn Bennett wasn't sure. The President was alive, but for how long?

And if he became a hostage of these terrorists, would he still be commander in chief?

*Chapter Thirteen*_____

Dispatched by Korshunov to see what had become of Bazylev and his search of the lower deck, Sergei Lenski descended the winding metal staircase down into the front lower galley.

From the shadows beyond the galley, Marshall gripped a machine-gun pistol in both hands and watched the terrorist coming down in the shaft of light from the upper deck; moving cautiously forward, ready to pick off another adversary and improve his odds, Marshall saw his prey—who had come upon the body of his comrade on the galley floor—scurry back up the stairs, shoes pinging on metal.

The light shaft disappeared to the accompaniment of a thud; and when Marshall, almost running into the galley, found his way in the near darkness to the bottom of the stairs, he was looking up at the access panel, put back in place, closing off the lower deck.

Marshall swore, silently; that hatch would be secure and/or guarded now, and was of no further use to him.

They had him sealed off down here. If they were smart, they'd send no more men down for him to systematically eliminate. What harm could he do them, locked away in the baggage hold with the other luggage? The dumbwaiters in both lower galleys were jammed as well.

I have to get this goddamn plane on the ground, Marshall thought, feeling stymied, glancing around, noticing a stream of milk from a bullet-pierced carton leaking through the busted glass door of the refrigerator.

Flush with the idea the wound of white had given him, he hurried out of the galley, knowing the true innards of the plane, the avionics compartment, would be somewhere beyond, possibly behind a panel.

This time he didn't have to call information. He hit Redial on the phone and got patched right through. And General Greely himself connected him with Chief Mechanic Jerry Foreman, 89th Air, who said, "This is an honor, Mr. President, though I believe we both wish the circumstances were different."

"That's a safe assumption, Jerry."

"What can I do for you, sir?"

"You can help me dump some fuel off this baby."

And Chief Mechanic Foreman, speaking from a hangar at Andrews Air Force Base, guided Marshall to a panel adjacent to the left wing of the plane, where (using the nose of the MP-5, a screwdriver being unavailable), the President of the United States grunted and groaned until he had popped the damn thing open and stepped into the claustrophobic compartment, where a service light had gone automatically on.

"It's a little more complicated than the old days," Marshall commented over his satellite phone.

And Chief Mechanic Foreman said, "It's not exactly like lifting up the hood of a Subaru, is it, sir?"

He was in a cramped world of electronics—bundled

wires and circuit boards and steel conduits and maintenance panels, one of which was clearly marked FUEL SYSTEM.

"Listen, Jerry, your signal's getting weak, breaking up," Marshall said. "It's going to take me a minute to get this panel off. . . . I've instructed the general to keep this line directly patched to you."

"Understood, sir. I'll wait for your call."

And Marshall, blinking sweat from his eyes, feeling the pain of the workingman as one of his predecessors never truly had, pushed End on the portable phone and moved back to the galley, to find a kitchen knife to pry the damn panel open.

On the upper deck, in the Mission Communications Center, the glowing blinks of electronics flashing on his face as if reflecting his thoughts, Korshunov grumbled and paced, grumbled and paced. Lenski had just told him of finding Bazylev butchered in the lower galley.

"After all our planning, all our training, overcoming odds no others had ever dared, to have our goal, our noble goal . . . jeopardized by one man? One renegade government lackey? Not acceptable . . . not acceptable . . ."

"We've cut him off," Lenski said, gesturing with open hands. "What damage can he do us now?"

Korshunov raised a lecturing finger and smiled. "Let us not underestimate our adversary, however much contempt we may have for what he represents. One infiltrator, one dedicated soldier raiding after dark, can defeat an army. Have you forgotten that saying of our youth?" And in Russian, Korshunov said, "Bless a bear with enough bee stings, he will lie down and die."

Lenski nodded.

In their seats of honor along one wall, Grace Marshall, who had taken a rather nasty tumble during the shock wave, was being comforted by her daughter, for a change. Korshunov halted his pacing and his gaze fell upon his guests; and he began to smile.

"That intercom," Korshunov asked Nevsky. "Can we send it down to the lower deck? So our noble adversary can hear us?"

"Certainly," Nevsky said.

"An amusing notion occurs to me," Korshunov said, and he conferred with the two freedom fighters, keeping his words from the First Lady and her daughter, not wanting to spoil the surprise he had in mind.

Sick with fear, trembling as if with palsy, Melanie Mitchell was escorted by Nevsky from the conference room, up the hallway, to the circular stairway that led to the upper deck. Nevsky joined his compatriot Lenski at the foot of those stairs and in gentlemanly fashion gestured for Melanie to go on up, which she did, unattended. The two freedom fighters admired the sight of her slender, shapely legs as she ascended; they exchanged shrugs as Sergei lifted the carpeted floor panel over the stairway into the lower-deck galley, light washing down and illuminating the feet of the dead Bazylev below.

Korshunov met the deputy press secretary at the door, ushering her in graciously. "Come, my dear, come."

He took her arm, guiding her inside the Mission Communications Center, where Grace and Alice Marshall looked at her with sympathy and dismay. Melanie felt somewhat reassured by Korshunov's manner; after all, they had hit it off, hadn't they, when she had shown him around the plane? There'd been a chemistry . . . hadn't there?

"My dear, I thought I'd ask you to join our little party," Korshunov began, showing her to a seat positioned before the microphone that fed the plane's public-address system; the mike sat on a little stand on a shallow counter by a control panel. "It's starting to feel a little lonesome up here. . . . Speak into the microphone, if you would."

"All right."

Her voice echoed across the ship—including the lower deck, where Marshall, on his way back from the galley with a knife to pry open the fuel-supply maintenance panel, was startled—first by the voice, which he immediately recognized as Melanie Mitchell's, and then by the shaft of light behind him in the galley, now, indicating that the hatch panel had been lifted. . . .

In the Mission Communications Center, Korshunov was passing the microphone from himself to Melanie, like the host of a talk show going out into the audience. Of course, David Letterman didn't usually have a machine pistol in his other hand, pointed at his guest.

"State your name, dear, would you?" he asked pleasantly. "For the record?"

"Melanie . . . Melanie Mitchell."

"And you're the deputy press secretary?"

"Yes . . . yes."

"You were very professional, very courteous to us, when we boarded the plane. Thank you."

"You . . . you're welcome."

On the lower deck, standing on the gangway near the

opened hatch of the avionics compartment, President James Marshall stood frozen. Listening. And watching that shaft of light.

In the Mission Communications Center, Grace Marshall could not bear to look at this absurd parody of an interview, the man with the microphone and gun, the poor quavering young woman. . . .

Korshunov asked, "You travel often with the President?"

"Yes I do."

"So, you're acquainted with everyone on the plane."

"I . . . I would say so."

"And I'm sure you're a popular young woman. Attractive, pleasant. You've made friendships."

"I suppose."

"Even with the Secret Service agents? Or are they too cold? Too professional?"

"They're nice people."

Korshunov smiled pleasantly, rose, and put his machine pistol to her head. "Oh, but you are trembling. . . . Why are you afraid, Miss Mitchell?"

"Because . . . because I don't want to die."

"And tell me, dear, what is it I'm doing at this very moment?"

"You're . . . you're pointing a gun at me."

"Ah, yes. I would seem to be. Thank you, Melanie." The cordial tone shifted into something harder-edged. "And now I'm speaking to the Secret Service agent in the baggage deck."

And the voice boomed in Marshall's ears, as he leaned against the bulkhead, feeling tired, so tired: *"I will count to ten. If you do not surrender before I reach ten, this pleasant young woman will die."*

And Melanie's sob: *"No . . ."*

Marshall's legs felt rubbery; he slumped to the gang-way, and sat, and listened to the awful countdown.

"One . . . two . . . three . . ."

In the conference room, hostages huddled, some stony-faced, others weeping, all tortured by the anticipation of the next atrocity.

". . . four . . ."

Lenski and Nevsky, machine pistols in hand, stood by the opening in the floor that looked down on the galley and the feet of their dead friend; patiently, they waited and aimed the weapons downward.

". . . five . . ."

Marshall knew that to surrender would betray every-thing he believed in, and very likely lose any chance to save the other hostages. But could he allow Melanie to be shot down like an animal? Nausea coursed through him . . . an awful sickness. . . .

". . . six . . ."

And in the Mission Communications Center, Korshunov held his weapon to the woman's head. Melanie's tears were streaming as she bit her lip and silently, des-perately, prayed.

". . . seven," Korshunov said.

Grace Marshall almost screamed, "You can't do this!"

And on the lower deck, Marshall—elated and destroyed by the sound of his wife's voice, his wife alive—heard first Korshunov say, *"Eight,"* and then Grace again: *"Let me talk to him! Let me talk to the agent!"*

His wife's voice ringing in his ears, tears clouding his eyes but not his judgment, the President rose to his feet slowly, in a shambling manner, though quite steady once he got to his feet.

Korshunov's voice rang through the lower deck: *". . . nine!"*

And Marshall, turning his back on the shaft of light and his wife's voice *("Oh, God, no!")* entered the avionics compartment, machine pistol in one hand, kitchen knife in the other. He shut his eyes, as if it would all go away.

On the Mission Communications Deck, Melanie Mitchell turned to look at the bearded, boyish face of Ivan Korshunov and she gave him the saddest smile any human ever smiled as she beseeched him to show her some pity, to remember how they had connected, their chemistry. . . .

"Ten," Korshunov said, and, with a single round of his machine pistol, the chemistry of Melanie Mitchell's brain ceased to function.

On the lower deck, the gunshot still echoing over the speakers, Marshall—in the midst of prying off that maintenance panel—shuddered as if the bullet had hit him.

But it hadn't.

It had shattered the skull and exploded the brain and ended the life of Melanie Mitchell, who tumbled from her chair, a tragic paragraph in a forthcoming news release.

Grace Marshall covered her daughter's eyes with one hand even as she gathered the girl to her, and both of them were screaming, and weeping.

That sound, too, was playing over the PA, and Marshall—his family's agony in his ears—studied the bundled wires and circuit boards before him, and tried to concentrate on them, and ignore the voice echoing through the lower deck.

*"Let us pause to contemplate what has just happened,
shall we? And, in a while, we'll repeat the exercise.
Only next time, I promise to choose someone . . . more
important."*

Lenski and Nevsky replaced the panel in the floor,
again sealing off the lower deck, the shaft of light into
the galley cutting off like a switch had been thrown.

But Marshall didn't notice; he was busy.

The hideous thudding and clunking of Melanie Mitchell's body being dragged from the Mission Communications Center and down the stairs, like so much meat,
provided a dreadful accompaniment to Grace Marshall's
rebukes: "You bastard! You heartless goddamn fucking
bastard!"

"Such language before the young ears of your daughter," the terrorist scolded mildly. "Besides, the Secret
Service agent killed that young woman, not me. Pity."

Alice was weeping and Grace was doing her best to
comfort the child, stroking her hair, patting her back as if
she were much younger, there there, there there . . . but
as she performed these gentle acts, Grace glared at Korshunov with all the hatred she could summon.

It didn't escape his notice.

He laughed silently, humorlessly, and said, "Yours is
not a difficult mind to read, First Lady. No tarot cards are
required. You wish me dead. Well, it may come to that.
In a war, soldiers die."

"This isn't a war," Grace said, and nodded toward the
smear of blood on the floor, "and she wasn't a soldier.
Just an innocent unarmed civilian."

Now his laugh rattled the room. "You! You who murder a hundred thousand Iraqis to save a few cents per gallon of gas. . . . You are going to lecture *me* on the morality of war? Don't *dare* insult me in this manner!" He waved her off, snorting his disgust, muttering, "You Americans are soft."

Arm around her daughter, holding her close, Grace gave him as condescending a smile as she could muster. "How do you think your grand plan is working out so far?"

He snorted again, a laugh. "You are in an odd position to sit in judgment of that."

"I don't think so," Grace said, stroking her daughter's hair. "You're the one losing control. Losing your men, one by one. Shooting hostages . . ."

"This only shows our resolve!"

"It only makes it easier for my husband to say no to your demands."

Korshunov pointed the weapon at her, but it was only a gesture. "Your husband could finish this with one phone call! One phone call, and General Radek would be released, and then, so would you! Why does he not do this?"

"Because he could never do business with a beast like you," she replied.

Korshunov seemed about to hit her again, possibly with the side of the weapon, when Alice looked up suddenly and said, "No! Please don't. . . ."

And he didn't.

Grace didn't know it, but she had been saved a punishing blow by her daughter's resemblance to the terrorist's own middle child, in a Kazakhstan city not so far away now, from the path of Air Force One.

In the conference room where shell-shocked hostages tried to absorb the tragedy of Melanie Mitchell's death even as it mingled with the selfish relief each sensed, the President's most trusted inner circle had gathered in one corner—chief of staff, Secret Service, military.

Lloyd Shepherd was pissed off. "Jesus, Gibbs—who the hell is down there on that baggage deck? That Russian said it was Secret Service. *Who* in hell?"

"I don't know," Gibbs said. "I presumed any agents not in this room were dead. Apparently I was wrong."

Shepherd waggled a finger at the Secret Service agent. "Melanie Mitchell was murdered because one of your hotshots wouldn't show himself. I want to know who that son-of-a-bitch is! He's endangering us all!"

"Hell, I'd like to know myself," Gibbs admitted.

"Sir," Major Caldwell said to Shepherd, "whoever's down there is smart enough to know that if you're hunting with one bullet, you wait for the right shot."

Shepherd smirked. "What the hell's that supposed to mean?"

"It means," Caldwell said, "that the 'son-of-a-bitch' down in baggage is very likely our best and only hope."

"Our only hope is that Washington complies with the terrorist demands," Shepherd said, "because any minute now, another one of us is going to die. And you know what? I'm not anxious for it to be me."

"Then I would suggest we organize ourselves," the major said, "and rush them. We outnumber them. They can't shoot all of us, and that'd be preferable to being led off to slaughter, one by one."

"Are you crazy?" Shepherd asked, and it didn't seem all that rhetorical. "I'll be no part of that!"

"Then with all due respect, sir," Major Caldwell said, "shut the fuck up."

In the claustrophobic avionics compartment, Marshall was back on the phone with Chief Mechanic Jerry Foreman, 89th Air (who was hunkered with several of his staff members over the schematics of the 747-200, back at Andrews Air Force Base).

Marshall, phone in the cradle of his chin and neck, said, "I have removed the maintenance panel."

"Good," Foreman said. "You should see a red toggle switch."

"I do."

"Well, toggle it up."

"Hang on. We've got some indicator lights goin' on, here."

"That only means you're aerated. No prob."

"Good."

"Now, Mr. President, to dump the fuel, you have to close the circuit for the pump."

"Isn't there a switch?"

"Sorry, no. So you'll have to cross the wires. Didn't you ever hot-wire a car in your youth?"

"Don't believe everything the Democrats tell you, Jerry."

"I never do, sir. You're dealing with a man who voted for you."

"That's a relief, at least. Point me to these wires."

"Open the fuel-control door, Mr. President. There should be five wires."

"Don't see 'em . . . wait—here to my left?"

"Exactly."

"I've got green, yellow, red, white, and blue."

"Okay, hang on," the mechanic said, but his voice was breaking up; the line was getting staticky.

"Losing you, Jerry! Hurry up! Jesus . . ."

"Sir, if you get the wrong wire, you'll cut the engine feeds."

"Meaning?"

"Meaning . . . the plane will crash."

"Oh, well, that's pretty much how my day's been going. So by all goddamn means, let's find the right fucking wire."

"First, cut—"

But the static made the rest unintelligible.

"Again, Jerry!" Marshall said. "You're breaking up!"

". . . green wire."

"Cut the green wire first?"

"Yes."

With his kitchen knife, Marshall cut the green wire; but in his ear, the static was increasing, the phone batteries dying. . . .

"It's cut, it's cut, what next?"

"Cross it with the . . . wire. . . ."

"Hello?"

The static was gone now. Jerry was gone. Everything was gone.

Marshall kept trying. "Hello, Jerry? Goddamnit, hello? Are you still there?"

But the phone was as dead as everyone on this plane

would be if he made the wrong choice among these remaining wires: yellow, red, white, blue.

Cross the green wire with what? he wondered, and he stared at the wires, looking for a message, a sign, anything.

The patriotic choice was obvious: he had to leave the red, white, and blue unsullied, didn't he? He would cut the yellow wire. Which he did, with his kitchen knife, and then he spliced it with the green. . . .

The engines groaned, as if they were coming to a stop.

But they weren't.

And under Air Force One, a trickle of gasoline turned quickly into a strong, steady stream.

In the cockpit of his F-15 Eagle, Colonel Frank Carlton, hearing himself say something else he'd never expected to say, reported back to a relieved Situation Room at the White House that Air Force One was indeed dumping fuel.

Chapter
Fourteen_____

Korshunov hustled from the Mission Communications Center into the cockpit, summoned by a disturbing yelp of dismay from his pilot.

Leaning over the copilot's chair, Korshunov asked, "What is it, Andrei?"

"Shit," Kolchak said, fingers flying over instruments but just touching them, adjusting nothing, a desperate faith healer, "we're losing fuel!"

A red warning light flashed insistently on the control panel, flushing their faces with a scarlet pulse.

Korshunov dropped into the copilot seat. "How in hell? What have you done?"

"Nothing! But fuel level's dropping down, fast ... wait."

"What?"

Kolchak's eyes were fixed on a gauge. "Avionics compartment. Shit, we aren't losing fuel, we're *dumping* fuel! That Secret Service agent has gotten into the avionics system, he's dumping our goddamn fuel!"

"Bastard!" A grunt of anger rose from Korshunov's chest. "So we have him safely sealed off, do we? With access to the electronics of this ship, we have him sealed off. Clever bastard, more clever than we are, I'm afraid. What's our status?"

Kolchak gestured helplessly toward his instrument panel, the red pulse continuing. "Even if we could stop this now, we do not have enough fuel to reach Kazakhstan airspace. We don't have enough fuel to make it home."

"But if we don't stop this . . ."

Kolchak swallowed, and gave his comrade a desperate look, his face pale when it wasn't red from the pulsing warning light. "Crash landing—or just crash."

"*Can* you stop this?"

He was thinking, thinking. "If I could get to that avionics compartment, I could. On the lower deck. Where *he* is . . ."

Korshunov frowned. "Can't we send Igor instead, or Sergei?"

"No," Kolchak said, and, engaging autopilot with the flick of a thumb, climbed out of the pilot's seat. "I'm the only one with the knowledge. I have to go."

Korshunov gripped the arm of his second-in-command as the man moved between the two seats. "Go, then," he said, "but take Sergei with you. You be careful! Without you, we have no pilot."

"If I don't do this," Kolchak said, "we have no plane."

And he was gone, leaving Korshunov in the copilot seat, a passenger at the wheel.

Sergei Lenski, waiting as Kolchak opened the floor panel exposing the stairwell into the lower front galley, glanced down the hallway, where Igor Nevsky paced before the door of the conference room, machine pistol cradled in his hands.

"If it isn't us coming up out of this rabbit hole," Lenski called to his hawkish friend, "blow his head off."

Nevsky nodded.

Kolchak was starting down the stairs, and Lenski followed. They moved past their fallen comrade, the stench of death intermingling with food smell, their feet crunching on the shattered glass of the broken refrigerator door, no doubt signaling the Secret Service renegade who hid somewhere in the semidarkness of the baggage deck.

"I can feel his eyes on us," Kolchak whispered, then took the lead, moving at a fast clip down the gangway, toward the middle of the plane, as Lenski hustled behind him, silently sweeping the area with the snout of his weapon.

Something moved in the darkness, down toward the wing section, and Lenski fired past Kolchak, letting a burst of MP-5 fire light up the world in blossoms of orange, and then the world blossomed back at them, as a captured MP-5 in the intruder's hands returned orange death in their direction, Lenski taking a round in the shoulder, just missing the assault vest, and it was like someone had shoved him, wet warmth following, and he dropped to one knee and kept firing as Kolchak ducked into an opening in the wall.

Gunfire exploding like a thunderstorm just outside his doorless door, Kolchak—tucked away in the cramped avionics compartment—looked around, at first overwhelmed by the nest of bundled wires, conduits, and panels; but then his eyes narrowed, and he selected a panel, pried it quickly open with his combat knife, the battle raging steps away from him resounding in his ears.

Lenski, having ducked behind a strut, was bobbing in

and out, returning fire, still lacking a true bead on his target, responding instinctively to the bursts of gunfire from the near darkness down the gangway.

The intruder's gunfire was unending; he apparently had more than one MP-5 or at least had looted Bazylev's body for his spare magazines.

Now Lenski's clip was empty.

And the rain of bullets continued, accompanied by the thunder of the intruder's fusillade. Lenski got down low and scooted across the gangway, rounds zinging overhead, gunfire echoing in this metal landscape, his left arm a throbbing aching useless bloody mess.

Kolchak, in the process of ripping wiring from a panel, looked over his shoulder at his fellow freedom fighter crawling in, and said, "You've been hit."

"How much longer?"

"A few more minutes."

"I need a new magazine."

Kolchak plucked one from his assault-vest pocket and tossed it to him. "Don't go out there—position yourself by the opening."

Lenski slammed in the fresh clip. "He could pin us down in here."

"Better than pick you off out there. When I'm finished with this, we'll be two men with weapons moving fast."

"He's a goddamn ghost."

Kolchak was combining wires, making them spark and burn, an acrid smell wafting through the little compartment.

"Not till we kill him, he isn't," Kolchak said, and his fingers nimbly selected more wires to jerk loose from their moorings.

* * *

At the sound of gunfire from the deck below, Igor Nevsky left his post at the conference-room door and moved to the open hatchway behind the winding stairs to the upper deck. He could see nothing down there but the feet of the late Boris Bazylev, in the spotlightlike shaft of light the open hatchway provided.

Nevsky called down, in Russian: "Are you all right?"

No response.

The gunfire let up, at least momentarily, and Nevsky called down again, "Sergei! Kolchak! What's happening?"

A voice in Russian called up: "The intruder is dead. Come give us a hand."

"Finally," Nevsky said to himself, slung his MP-5 on its strap over his shoulder, and started down the steps.

In the Situation Room at the White House, Vice-President Kathryn Bennett and Secretary of Defense Walter Dean were on their feet, studying the tactical wall map that luminously revealed Air Force One's southwest path toward Kazakhstan.

The Vice President was again speaking to the terrorist leader who held Air Force One, his voice loud and chillingly distinct in the overhead speakers.

"Madame Vice-President," the voice said, oozing false charm, *"the time has come for you to demonstrate your good faith. I have been reading the press kit provided me by the thoughtful, and unfortunately deceased, Ms. Mitchell. Such a remarkable plane, your Air Force One—a super-plane, flying through mushroom clouds, evading missiles . . . even refueling in midair."*

"You have a need for fuel?" she asked dryly.

"I suggest you not play cat and mouse with me, Madame

Vice-President, because it is the cat who has the hostage mice. . . . We need fuel, and we need it immediately."

Her voice was as cordial as if she were chatting at a country-club cocktail party: "I'm sure we can strike some sort of arrangement. Land the plane and we'll trade you fuel for our people. We're even willing to allow you to land at a Kazakhstan base to do so."

"You know very well that we will not have sufficient fuel by that time. Under no circumstances will I trade hostages for fuel."

"In most bargains, each side gives something to the other."

"Enough bullshit. Do you understand simple physics? Without fuel, the plane crashes. The plane crashes, everybody dies."

Bennett paused, glanced at Dean, who shrugged; then she said, "We will give you the fuel in return for an extension of time for us to arrange the release of General Radek. We ask for three hours during which you will harm no hostages."

"Ah. You wish to haggle. Very well. Dickering in the marketplace is an old Russian custom. Assure me that my fuel is on its way to me, right now, or I will execute a member of your senior staff . . . and I will continue killing hostages not at the rate of one per half hour, Madame Vice-President, but of one every minute—until we crash or until a refueling plane arrives."

Again Bennett looked at Dean; she raised an eyebrow, and he sighed and nodded.

"The fuel is on its way," she said.

"Thank you. A pleasure doing business with you."

The click of the terrorist cutting himself off was hardly

over before General Greely was on the horn, issuing the order. Bennett turned to Dean with a wry smile.

"And I thought we finally had something to cut a deal with."

Dean sighed and his smirk was humorless. "And I thought my ex-wife's lawyer was tough."

Within the avionics compartment, Kolchak took a step back and regarded his handiwork: scorched, torn wires, at precisely selected junctures.

"I burned the circuits," he said to Lenski, who crouched at the compartment opening, weapon at the ready. "No chance of our friend doing that again."

And through the hatchway in the galley, echoing like the voice of God, using his lungs not the PA, came Korshunov's bellow: "Refueling plane on its way!"

"Good, very good," Kolchak said.

"Can we *go* now?" Lenski asked.

"Nothing pressing keeping us here."

"On three . . ."

Softly, Lenski counted, and soon, in one quick fluid motion, they were out of the avionics compartment and onto the gangway, Kolchak firing his MP-5 blindly ahead of him as he sprinted toward the forward galley, Lenski bringing up the rear, running backward, firing into the rear of the plane, spraying the perimeter wildly, bullets ricocheting off metal and sinking softly into baggage, the deck reverberating with the rumble of gunfire, all but drowning out the roar of the huge jet engines.

Then the two Russians were scrambling through the galley and skirting their dead comrade Boris and clambering up the metal stairs to the main deck.

"Better get that tended to," Kolchak said to Lenski, whose upper left arm was a sodden red mess, using his right hand to shove that floor panel shut again, to seal off the hell below, and the devil who inhabited it.

Lenski got to his feet, looking down at the closed floor panel, nodding, saying, "Ivan's got first aid upstairs."

They were heading up the stairs to the upper deck and Mission Communications Control when they noticed Nevsky, standing awkwardly by the forward galley, rather than at his conference-room station.

"Everything all right?" Lenski asked him.

"Da," Nevsky said.

"I think we've got him contained," Kolchak said. "Better get back to your post."

"Da," Nevsky said.

And the two freedom fighters went into Mission Communications Control, to report their triumph and get some bandages for a wounded hero.

Moments later, Nevsky unlocked the conference room and stepped inside; the first thing the hostages noticed was the terrorist's lack of a gun.

The second thing they noticed was the President of the United States, James Marshall, stepping in behind him, nudging the terrorist with his own weapon.

Marshall shut the door, and stunned expressions turned joyful and the room became a shambles of surprise and celebration, hostages streaming from the walls and the table to crowd around a returning warrior, his shirt dirty, torn, bloody, his face not much better.

Rather roughly, Marshall sat his hostage down in a

chair, then turned to respond to the dozens of questions, and outcries of "Jim!" tumbling over one another, much like the friends and coworkers of his who were surrounding him, pushing in toward him, now.

Lloyd Shepherd moved to the forefront; his expression was that of a man struck from behind with a plank. "I don't understand . . . you escaped . . . what the hell are you doing here?"

"I never left," he said, "but they don't know that."

Major Caldwell, grinning, said, "*You're* the renegade agent!"

"Gibbs," Marshall said, handing a pistol he'd liberated from the terrorist to the Secret Service agent, "watch the door."

"Yes sir," Gibbs said, moving to that position with gun in hand.

Marshall fixed a hard gaze on his chief of staff. "Where's my family?"

Shepherd's expression was glum. "We haven't seen or heard anything of them since the terrorists took them out of here right after, uh . . . sir, I'm afraid Jack Doherty was executed."

"I'm aware of that."

Shepherd blinked. "You are?"

"The Vice-President told me."

The chief of staff was confused to the point of stupidity, as his response well indicated: "Is *she* on the ship?"

"No," Marshall snapped. "I made contact with her using your satellite phone; but the battery's dead now. We're out of contact."

"Sir," Caldwell said, "now that we have some weapons, not to mention strength of numbers, shouldn't we be moving toward retaking the plane?"

"I'd say yes," Marshall said, sighing wearily, sitting on the edge of the conference table, "if Grace and Alice weren't still in those bastards' hands."

"Sir, what about disabling the plane?" Shepherd asked. "Forcing them to land?"

"I tried that," Marshall said. "By dumping some fuel. But I heard the sons-of-bitches talking; they've convinced Washington to refuel 'em in midair."

Caldwell considered that information; then he said, "Well, if we're not going to take action, let's get our people the hell off this plane."

Marshall looked at the major, amazed. "That's possible?"

Caldwell nodded matter-of-factly. "We have emergency parachutes in the tail cone, lower deck, with a launch ramp. . . . But, sir, we're too damn high."

"Thirty thousand feet," Marshall said, and made a click in his cheek. "Air's too thin. You'd asphyxiate before hitting ground."

"Yes," Caldwell said, "but if we could get a message to the refueling tanker, and get 'em to have our hosts take the plane down to fifteen thousand feet, supposedly for refueling purposes, *then* we could jump."

Marshall was shaking his head no. "Major, they've disabled all the phones . . . they control the radios. And the portable's dead as hell."

Stepping forward, Janet Reynolds, an attractive black woman in her late twenties, a secretary assigned to the AFO in-flight office, offered a suggestion.

"Mr. President, if I may . . ." she began, tentative, embarrassed.

"Yes, Janet?"

"What about the fax machines?"

"The phones are out, I said."

"But, sir, the voice lines and faxes are on two different systems of encryption . . . it's a security thing. If you disabled one line, it would be real easy to overlook the other, particularly if you were an outsider and didn't know exactly how we had things set up here. If I'm not out of line, you know, mentioning this . . ."

Marshall beamed and put two hands on the woman's shoulders, as if he were knighting her. "Janet, you're not only *not* out of line, if you're right, you may become the youngest postmaster general in our nation's history. You want to come down to the office and show me?"

She beamed back at him. "Absolutely."

Marshall turned to Major Caldwell. "Give me a few seconds, and then start getting our people down to the lower deck. You know where the hatch is? Behind the flight-deck stairway?"

Caldwell nodded.

"Take care," Marshall told him. "Run silent, run deep— the terrorists are up in Mission Communications. If they hear you, and a firefight breaks out . . ."

"Understood, sir."

Marshall turned to his constituency. "People, when you move through the lower galley, you're going to trip over a dead terrorist. So if you're squeamish, get over it, now." He put a hand on Caldwell's shoulder and whispered, "Might give 'em a quick prepping . . . They haven't exactly trained as paratroopers."

Caldwell raised his eyebrows and set them back down. "Affirmative on that, sir . . . and remember: fifteen thousand feet . . . oh, and two hundred knots! Otherwise, it's suicide."

"Staying is suicide," Marshall said, and he handed one of his MP-5s to Caldwell. "You may need this."

"Yes, sir," Caldwell said.

"Gibbs," the President said, "you might want to position our friend here"—he nodded toward the seated hostage—"in that hallway so that it looks like he's still on guard, if somebody peeks out of the upper deck, checking on us."

"Yes, sir," Gibbs said, moving from the door and training the weapon on the seated Russian. "Good luck, sir."

"Good luck to all of us."

Stepping into the hallway, Marshall held his machine pistol out in front of him, like a flashlight searching through darkness. All was quiet; empty. He and Janet Reynolds ran down the hall and into the office.

The President quickly went to a desk, found a pen, and began to write out his message.

"The faxes appear operational," she said. "Where are we sending it?"

He handed her the sheet of paper. "Situation Room. I hope you know the number."

"By heart, sir," she assured him. "Sir, I just want to say it makes me proud to be a small part of this effort. And how proud I am that you stayed here, with us, to help us . . . no matter how this comes out."

And the secretary slipped the sheet into the feed of the fax machine, which whined, and began slowly sucking the paper through, sending its transmission to Washington, D.C.

She looked at him with glee. It was working!

And the President smiled back at her. "Thank *you*, Madame Postmistress."

Then, like a couple of kids who'd just gotten away with a prank, they ran into the hallway, where the exodus of the passengers was under way. Major Caldwell, a machine pistol in hand, was positioned by the circular stairway to the upper deck. Gibbs was holding the captive terrorist in the forward galley, at gunpoint.

And the hostages—a few at a time—were sneaking down the corridor, toward the steps, then disappearing around the stairs and down into the lower deck.

Mice sneaking into their little hole, past a cat.

Just as hostages were exiting the conference room on the flying White House, the deputy national security adviser was ushering the attorney general of the United States into the Situation Room of the real one. No one was yet aware that a fax from AFO had just spilled out of a machine into a bin.

Tom Lee announced Attorney General Andrew H. Ward, drawing Vice-President Bennett and Defense Secretary Dean away from the wall map where they were mesmerized, watching the progress of Air Force One as it moved toward Kazakhstan airspace.

The corpulent sixty-year-old, owlish attorney general lumbered over to shake hands with Bennett, who said, "Andrew, thank you for coming so quickly."

Ward was not one for amenities; he cut directly to the heart of the matter: "I've been told you want my interpretation of what the Constitution has to say about this matter."

"That's correct," Bennett said.

"Our founding fathers didn't exactly anticipate this particular circumstance, of course. . . ."

"Andrew," Dean said, "my understanding is that if the President is out of contact, in a military situation, the secretary of defense steps in, as second-in-command."

Ward seemed almost bored. "Yes, of course."

Dean smiled tightly, clapped his hands once. "I'm glad to have that settled."

"It's not settled at all," Ward said, and he plodded over to a chair at the conference table and settled his massive weight into it. Bennett and Dean hovered at his either side, neither taking a seat.

"What do you mean?" Bennett asked.

"The President is not merely out of contact, he is under duress, his family held hostage, and he may possibly be a hostage himself. We're no longer in contact with him?"

"No," Bennett said.

"His portable phone batteries gave out," Dean explained.

"Well," Ward sighed, "this clearly creates an incapacity to discharge the office under the Twenty-fifth Amendment. This goes well beyond mere military considerations. He might just as well have had a stroke."

Now Dean sat down; this was not what he had hoped to hear.

Communications Officer Peters approached and whispered to Bennett, "Excuse the interruption, Madame Vice-President, but I thought you should know: CNN is broadcasting an unconfirmed report that Air Force One may have crashed in Eastern Europe."

"What?"

"They're saying the unconfirmed report has all fifty-some passengers dying, including the First Family."

"Christ," Bennett said. "Genie's out of the bottle. Call the press room. I'll make a statement.

"Excuse me, gentlemen," the Vice-President said, and walked briskly from the room.

And the fax remained unnoticed in its bin.

Chapter Fifteen_____

In the White House Press Room, Bruce Gleason, assistant press secretary (not knowing his immediate superior, Melanie Mitchell, was now deceased), did his best to quell the questions of the baying hounds of the nation's news media.

"Has Air Force One crashed?" a *Washington Post* reporter wanted to know, but his question was barely out before the AP correspondent blurted, "Is the President alive or dead?", over which the NBC correspondent almost yelled, "What about the CNN reports of air-force personnel searching wreckage for the President's body in a farmer's field in Germany?"

Gleason, new at this—a thirty-year-old former *Des Moines Register* reporter who had begun to hate the media more than someone who didn't hold an MFA in journalism—adjusted his glasses with one hand and patted the air with the other.

"As far as I know," Gleason said, striving for a calm tone and achieving desperation, "those are all rumors, and no, I don't know where CNN got that story. I can't confirm anything—"

And arriving unannounced, moving briskly into the

room as her Secret Service entourage fanned out and took their places, the Vice-President of the United States walked from the side door and to the podium, nodding to Gleason to stand aside, which he gladly, gratefully did.

The din had increased at the sight of her, but now receded, as those reporters not already on their feet stood, in a hushed combination of respect and hunger.

Kathryn Bennett motioned for the press to be seated, and said, "Thank you, Bruce," as her audience settled into their seats, or rather onto the edge of them.

"Ladies and gentlemen," she went on in a somber but controlled manner, "I have a brief statement, after which I will not be answering questions. However, I believe you will shortly understand why I cannot spend much time with you here. . . . The President's plane, Air Force One, has been skyjacked. . . ."

A murmur crossed the crowd, momentarily, then the room fell to hear-a-pin-drop level as the Vice-President continued.

"For security reasons," she said, "I cannot divulge the identity of the hijackers or the names of those aboard the plane. There have been at least two casualties and family members will of course be notified before the media."

Another wave of whispering rippled across the room, then stopped as Bennett's voice picked up strength.

"I am here to assure the American people that we are doing everything in our power to resolve this situation. To say more would be to endanger our people. . . . Thank you."

But as Bennett moved away from the lectern, a murmuring evolved quickly into a tumult of questions, one on top of the other, as the hungry beasts leaped and snarled at any possibility of a tidbit being tossed their way. *Is the President on board, what about the First Family, what are the skyjackers' demands, who are the skyjackers, is the President a hostage, have you become acting president?*

With the video cams of the major television news services watching her every move, Bennett could not ignore the questions out of hand. She returned, tentatively, to the lectern and held up a single hand in a stop motion.

"For the safety of the people on the plane, I can't tell you any more than I already have," she said. "I will respond to one question, if it does not deal with the identities of our people aboard Air Force One."

And she singled out *The New York Times* correspondent, Peter Lewis, perhaps as a reward for the reporter maintaining a modicum of dignity.

"Is James Marshall still the President?" Lewis asked.

"Yes, James Marshall is still the President," she said, and a rush of relief passed across the room. "Pending his return, I am coordinating efforts with the National Security Council here at the White House. Thank you very much . . ."

But the questions began again, tumbling on top of each other, and Bennett returned to the microphone, and speaking in a voice that was at once that of a strict teacher and a loving parent, she said, "I want to assure the American people that we are working together to solve this problem. In the meantime, I would respectfully request that all Americans, no matter what their religious persuasion, pray for the safety of everyone on board Air Force One."

During the momentary surprise that followed this dramatic appeal, the questions of the media halting, the Vice-President of the United States made her way quickly out of the Press Room.

On Air Force One, the CNN satellite feed had been picked up via a monitor amid the elaborate electronics of the Mission Communications Center, and shared with an audience consisting of Ivan Korshunov, his comrade Sergei Lenski, and their two prize hostages, Grace and Alice Marshall.

But a grimacing Korshunov—cutting the sound on the feed—was soon pacing again, a stalking routine the room could barely contain. "Where is the goddamn *President*?"

"They have had more than sufficient time to recover him from the escape pod," Lenski said with a frown, then shrugged. "Perhaps he was injured."

"Perhaps," Korshunov said, not convinced. "If his injury were severe enough, they might conceal that. But she is hiding *something,* this Vice-President, this treacherous woman. Where *is* he?"

Holding her daughter's hand, Grace did her best to keep her expression impassive, even though a thought was forming, a notion so outrageous, so unlikely, and yet so very much like her husband. . . .

Korshunov tromped over to the blown-open cockpit door, stuck his head in, asking, "Anything?"

Kolchak shook his head. "No sign of the refueling plane yet, Ivan."

Grunting, Korshunov strode to the door above the stairway down to the main deck, stuck his head out. He saw Igor Nevsky standing near the galley, rather stiffly.

"Everything all right down there?"

"Da," Nevsky said.

"Why aren't you at your post? Get back to your post!"

Nevsky seemed to hesitate, and Korshunov was about to start down the stairs to see if something was wrong with him—perhaps the loss of two fellow freedom fighters was eating at the young man's nerves—when Kolchak's voice, echoing back from the cockpit across the Mission Communications Center, seized his attention.

"Ivan!" Kolchak was calling. "It's here! The refueling plane!"

And Korshunov retreated into the upper deck, leaving his heart-to-heart talk with Nevsky for later, rushing into the cockpit to join Kolchak, never having seen the handful of hostages just under his feet, below the winding stairway, by the open hatch to the lower deck into which they were escaping.

Marshall, on the lower deck, a world he knew well, was guiding his friends and coworkers along the gangway toward the tail cone of the plane, the hatchway standing open to receive them into the parachute launchramp compartment. There, the remaining handful of airforce security guards used their expertise to distribute the parachutes from the wall racks and get the packs properly strapped onto to these novice sky divers.

Major Caldwell was supervising, inspecting straps and buckles and lending moral support, sending his instant graduates to stand behind a yellow line on the floor once he'd checked them, and by the time Marshall got there, two neat lines were already formed.

The sight of his White House staffers, in their civilian clothes, girded into parachutes, was an absurd, almost amusing one; but mostly Marshall felt a swell of pride, mingled with relief, that the terrorists would be denied these victims.

"Folks, listen up!" Caldwell ordered, working his voice over the engine thrum. The major himself was not yet in a parachute, and he used Janet Reynolds for his demonstration, pointing to various hooks and straps on her pack. "Remember, this is your main rip cord. . . . When you clear the plane, count to three and give it a yank. If your chute doesn't open, pull this loop, it's called a lollipop . . . that's your reserve chute."

"And if *it* doesn't open?" someone asked.

"It'll open," Caldwell said. "It'll open."

The launch-ramp control panel wasn't very complicated, consisting mostly of an emergency lever behind safety glass, a device no more complex than a fire alarm; but the panel did include an altimeter gauge, and Marshall stood studying the obstinate indicator, which still hovered around thirty thousand feet. "Your chute, sir," Caldwell said, handing the pack toward Marshall.

The President raised a hand in a little dismissive wave, as if declining an after-dinner mint.

"Sir?"

"I'm not going without my family. . . . Anyway, the point may be moot."

Caldwell, eyeing the sorry altimeter reading, nodded.

"We won't give our friend a chute, either," Marshall said, nodding toward the hawk-faced terrorist on whom Secret Service Agent Gibbs trained a gun. "I'll keep him as *my* hostage."

"You might be better off without him," Caldwell said. "But it's your call."

"You better get your chute on," Marshall said to the major. "Just in case we get lucky."

"If we do," Caldwell said, "I'll be staying with my president."

"Norm, that's not necessary."

"Yes, it is. Unless you order my ass off this plane, you've got some company."

Marshall shook the major's hand. "Glad to have it."

Then the President looked at that discouraging gauge and said, "Let's just hope we don't have the rest of these folks as company, as well."

But the needle stubbornly remained right at thirty thousand.

In the cockpit of AFO, where he had buckled himself into the copilot's chair, Korshunov's eyes were glued to another discouraging gauge: the fuel on the ship was very nearly gone.

The autopilot was engaged, but Kolchak sat in the captain's seat, ready to follow directions for refueling; however, the radio had fallen silent for some time. He sighed gloomily at Korshunov, shrugged helplessly, then suddenly the radio was alive in his headset. He gestured for Korshunov to put his headset on, too.

"Air Force One," the voice in the headsets was saying, "Air Force One, do you copy?"

"Yes, we read," Kolchak said. "Go ahead."

And suddenly a KC-135, a United States Air Force airborne gas station, glided right alongside of them, like two cars moving side by side down a one-way street.

"Air Force One," the voice in their headsets said, "this is Extender One-Zero. We have been instructed to refuel you, repeat, we have been instructed to refuel you."

"Go ahead," Kolchak said, disengaging autopilot, taking the wheel. "We are awaiting your instructions."

"Drop to fifteen thousand feet," the KC-135 pilot said, "and slow to two hundred knots."

"We acknowledge," Kolchak said. "Fifteen thousand feet, two hundred knots . . ."

And Kolchak eased up on the throttle, trading smiles with Korshunov. They had outwitted the Americans again.

In the tail cone on the lower deck of Air Force One, in the cramped chamber that housed the parachute launch ramp, Caldwell and Marshall stood watching the altimeter gauge as the two rows of impromptu paratroopers waited in line behind the yellow line. That their fate hinged upon what this gauge told them was not a secret: they had all heard Caldwell and Marshall discussing the need to drop to fifteen thousand feet, they all knew of the mission Marshall and Janet Reynolds had embarked upon, to get a fax sent to the Situation Room.

And it was Janet Reynolds, standing just opposite the gauge, who first said anything, even before Marshall or Caldwell, who were merely exchanging shit-eating grins.

"They got our fax!" she was shouting, jumping up and down like a kid at Christmas. "They got it, they got it!"

Lower and lower the needle dropped.

"Almost there," Caldwell said.

Marshall glanced at a small group of men gathered about him—Lloyd Shepherd, Secret Service Agent Gibbs (keeping the captive terrorist covered) and one of Gibbs's men, two air-force security guards—and noted that they, like Major Caldwell and himself, lacked parachutes. There were others available, on the metal racks on the curved walls.

"What about you guys?" Marshall asked. "Shouldn't you be getting dressed for the big dance?"

"Sir"—Gibbs glanced from face to face in the little group, of which he'd obviously been appointed spokesman—"we would like to stay with our president."

Marshall felt a wave of emotion and there was a quaver in his voice as he said, "Thank you, men. I'd be honored to have you stay here with me."

Quietly he sidled up to Shepherd and said, "Shep, are you sure about this? What about Kathy and the kids. . . ."

"I'm not proud of everything I've done tonight," Shep said. "But I do know one thing: as your chief of staff, I belong at your side. And, anyway . . . you have a family, too, don't you?"

Marshall put a hand on Shepherd's shoulder and squeezed.

Caldwell was at the control panel, hitting a switch, calling out, "Okay, everybody, relax—we're just depressurizing the compartment. This'll just take a few moments. . . ."

In the cockpit, Kolchak was following the instructions of the voice in his headset, Korshunov eavesdropping.

"Open your receptacle doors," the voice was saying.

"Done," Kolchak said.

"Pull the yellow lever."

"Which yellow lever?"

"It's on your upper control panel."

"I see it. It's done."

"Now, next to that lever there's a toggle switch, to open your intake. Got it?"

"Yes."

Suddenly, through the cockpit window, they saw the long metallic appendage dropping down from the tanker plane flying above them, the retractable metal tube that was the refueling boom, dangling down ahead of the plane like the leg of a silver insect.

"Air Force One," the voice said, "do you see the boom?"

"We see it," Kolchak said, startled, "we see it!"

"All right, close the distance, nice and easy. . . ."

And Kolchak edged the huge aircraft forward, ever so gently, toward that appendage; and, miraculously, the appendage found its groove and slid right in, two birds mating in flight.

Within the tail-cone compartment, with the KC-135 now flying directly above Air Force One, connected by a gas-line umbilical, the sound of the second plane's engines joined those of the 747's, creating a near-deafening mechanical hum.

Major Caldwell, watching the altimeter drop, yelled, "Close enough for government work!", and smashed the safety glass with the side of a fist, flicking away the glass shards, reaching in and pulling the lever. A mechanized whir was followed by a clank that gave way to a monstrous rush of wind as the tail section of the plane hinged open on hydraulic struts, extending behind the ship like a plank these parachuted hostages were being forced to walk, to drop into the endless black ocean of the nighttime sky, where gray streaky clouds floated like ghostly seaweed.

The churning wind, rushing by at two hundred knots, was a gale that whipped not just clothing, sending ties and dresses flapping, but virtually threatened to lift flesh off bone, distorting faces into living caricatures.

"Go!" Major Caldwell called out, and the first hostage dove into oblivion. "Go!" And another, and he kept prompting them, as more and more of the hostages on Air Force One took their chances with the sky and the night and a rip cord and a lollipop.

In the cockpit of Air Force One, as the silver umbilical hung beyond their window, a loud buzz drew the attention of Kolchak and Korshunov to a tactical video display on the control panel, where a diagram of the ship showing the ramp extending from the tail cone was accompanied by the words: EMERGENCY PARACHUTE RAMP ACTIVATING.

"What in the hell?" Korshunov said.

"Just a bug of some kind," Kolchak said, but he didn't sound sure.

"Sergei!" Korshunov called.

And Lenski, standing watch in the Mission Communications Center over the hostage First Family, leaned into the cockpit. "Yes, Ivan?"

"We may have an escape attempt," Korshunov said, loading his own weapon. He asked Kolchak, "Where would this 'emergency ramp' be located?"

Kolchak pointed to the display, and the image told the story, but the pilot interpreted nonetheless: "Tail of the plane, lower deck."

"Check the hostages," Korshunov ordered, and nodding toward the image on the computer monitor, he added, "then check that out. Take care—our Secret Service agent is still below."

Lenski nodded and hustled off, MP-5 in hand.

In the cockpit of his F-15, observing from a distance of several miles, Halo leader Colonel Frank Carlton was keeping Washington abreast of the operation's progress—the refueling diversion, and the parachutes blossoming from under the rear of the plane.

"So far ten chutes," Carlton said into his headset. He could hear the elation in the Situation Room back home, the Vice-President's voice saying, "Yes!"

And the white flowers continued blooming in the nighttime sky, Carlton reporting, "Fifteen parachutes, maybe twenty! Twenty chutes!"

Laughter and a sound that might have been a slap came over Carlton's headset; but it was not a slap, it was a sight few would have believed, had they seen it with their own eyes.

Because back in the Situation Room, the Vice-President and the secretary of defense had just shared a high five.

Sergei Lenski, finding the conference room empty, yelled up the stairs to the Mission Communications Center, "The hostages are gone!" but waited for no instructions from Korshunov. Lenski knew what he had to do; he clambered down the metal stairs into the lower-deck galley, MP-5 ready to spray death at anything in sight, leaping over dead Boris Basylev, who lay in a pool of blood and spilt milk, exiting the galley and sprinting down the gangway of the ship toward the tail cone, where he found the hatchway to the parachute launch ramp shut, tight, locked.

But through the porthole he could see them, the wind whipping them savagely, almost tearing the clothes off them, hostages with parachutes, jumping off the ramp and into the black sky, coached and prodded and aided by that major and several air-force security guards, and two Secret Service agents, and someone else, someone holding Nevsky hostage. . . .

The President!

The goddamn President of the United States was in that windy chamber, and it all made sense to Lenski, now—*Marshall* was the renegade, not some Secret Service agent! Marshall had never taken that pod, he'd sent it flying without a passenger, and stayed behind to sting and snipe from the shadows. . . .

And now the son-of-a-bitch was leading the hostages in an escape, even now the freedom fighters' bargaining chips were jumping off the ramp, into safety!

Lenski knew mere bullets wouldn't faze that steel hatch, and he looked around, thinking desperately, *What can I use? What can I use . . . ?*

In the rear galley he quickly found what he needed and he was grinning like a madman when he jammed the small tank of propane gas in the wheel of the hatch-door handle. He stepped away and aimed his machine pistol at the tank and fired a single round, exploding the tank, tearing the door off its hinges.

Another explosion immediately resulted, an explosion not of flame and smoke but of pressurized air, blasting the last few parachutists rather rudely into the night, and sending Igor Nevsky, who had the face of a hawk but not the wings, tumbling off the ramp as well, and into the dark endless sky, with only a scream for a parachute.

Marshall, too, went tumbling, sliding roughly down the ramp, even as weapons and unused parachutes also went sliding and flying into nowhere; but unlike the terrorist, he managed to grab hold of something, a hydraulic strut, and he dangled there, at the edge of the ramp, grasping with both arms, hugging on to it, with a hell of a view of those last few parachutists' chutes blossoming in the night, the wind tearing at him, and the ship itself bucking as that compartment suddenly depressurized, and bucking was right, because in holding on to that strut, Marshall felt he was riding the world's biggest pissed-off bronco.

The two air-force security guards, who had declined chutes and stayed with their president, now left him behind, losing their footing and tumbling off the platform. Marshall could not bear to watch the boys fall and he shut his eyes and held on and thought of Grace and Alice and he did not let fucking go, even though the plane did its damnedest to toss him off into that same bottomless sky those boys had gone screaming into, as if waking from a terrible nightmare into a worse living one.

In the cockpit of AFO, Kolchak was riding the same angry bronco, fighting the wheel as the huge plane quaked and jumped and flinched. In the copilot's seat, Korshunov was also quaking and shuddering and flinching, and in both of their ears came the sound of the KC-135 pilot, himself on the verge of panic.

"Air Force One," the voice cried into their headsets, "back off, back off! Back four, back six!"

The metallic tube out their window was shimmying, shifting. . . .

"I can't hold her!" Kolchak yelled into the headset, struggling with the wheel. "I can't hold her!"

"What the hell are you doing? Air Force One, break away, break away *now*!"

And Kolchak did, but not as the KC-135 pilot had intended, nor Kolchak, either; the ship jerked upward and to the side, and the metal tube dislodged and scraped harshly, gratingly, across the nose of the plane, cutting a gash in the metal with a sound that would make fingernails on a blackboard seem a symphony.

Only fingers on a blackboard don't create sparks.

And the sparks this scraping had created were jumping at the stream of gasoline pouring from that dislodged metal boom, igniting it into a stream of fire, the entire fueling arm engulfed in flame.

Eyes wide and orange with fiery reflection, Kolchak pushed the stick down and Air Force One went into a sharp, immediate dive; Korshunov did not have to be a trained pilot, or a rocket scientist either, to know what was coming and why Kolchak pushed at the throttle so urgently, and Korshunov's hands went onto the throttle, too, like boys using a baseball bat to choose sides, helping his pilot shove that stick forward.

Above them, of course, flames had traveled up into the tanker, a trail of fire that was a burning fuse on a flying bomb, which blew in a thunderous explosion that shook the sky and everything in it and much that was under it, creating a fire cloud that turned the night to instant noon.

Out of this temporary sun, this ball of flame, came drifting the burned-out skeleton of what had been the KC-135, emerging lazily and then suddenly falling toward the earth with an unwarranted urgency.

In his cockpit, Halo leader Colonel Carlton—and the other pilots in the F-15 escorts—found themselves flying toward a wall of flame.

"Everybody break!" Carlton called into his headset even as he followed his own orders. "Now! Now! Now!"

The F-15s went into an emergency climb, standing on their afterburners to escape the inferno where the sky used to be.

And the President of the United States—his eyes wide open now—was hanging from a strut of a diving plane, watching burning debris tumble around him like so many falling stars; the sky seemed to be raining fire.

From his front-row seat, the dangling President watched the charred fiery shell of the KC-135 perform a kamikaze dive, its flaming trail passing only a few hundred yards from him, the intensity of the heat on his flesh matched only by the angry howl of the gods in his ears and the pull of the plummeting plane on his fifty-year-old muscles.

Then the plane leveled out and the depressurized air began to subside, and Major Carlton, wind whipping his face, was reaching out to help him.

Only standing behind Carlton, hanging on to a strut with one hand, was that lean, dead-eyed terrorist, Lenski.

"Let him fall," the terrorist said.

"For God sakes," Caldwell was saying. Marshall could barely hear him over the two-hundred-knot wind. "He's the President of the United States! Think, man—he's your most valuable hostage!"

And then, under the watchful eye of the terrorist—and his machine pistol—Caldwell, Gibbs, and Shepherd formed a human link to crawl down the ramp so that Caldwell could extend his arms to Marshall, and reel him back into the ship.

Into the flying White House, his home sweet home in the sky.

In the AFO cockpit, Kolchak was steadying the plane.

"Fuel?" Korshunov asked him.

"Enough to get us home," Kolchak said with a smile.

"Home," Korshunov said, fondly.

"Home," Kolchak said, the same way.

*Chapter Sixteen*_____

In Washington, D.C., dusk was easing into night, the dying sun tracing orange streaks on the Potomac, the imposing monuments of a nation's heritage throwing long shadows, lights coming up on the pillars of democracy that were the columns of the house James Marshall called home—at least until November, next year.

Vice-President Kathryn Bennett and National Security Adviser Tom Lee, returning from having briefed the majority leaders of the House and Senate, entered the Situation Room, where Generals Northwood and Greely and Defense Secretary Dean stood before a towering luminous wall map as if it were an altar.

The general turned to them as they approached. He said, "We're counting thirty-two survivors. We've accounted for every parachute the F-15 pilots spotted jumping from Air Force One."

Bennett allowed herself a smile at this good news, but it dropped away as she said, "That means they've still got hostages."

"Yes it does."

"No word of the First Family?"

"None yet," Greely said.

Dean said, "Neither Grace nor Alice are among those we've recovered."

"Nice as this victory is," Bennett said, "it's only a partial one. Losing these hostages will only make the terrorists more desperate."

As if on cue, Communications Officer Peters called out: "Air Force One on the line!"

"Overhead," she instructed him, and the communications officer nodded.

Feet planted, as if ready for a body blow, Bennett said, "This is Vice-President Bennett. We're listening."

"Congratulations on regaining some of your countrymen. I applaud you for your ingenuity, but caution you not repeat any such acts of deceit."

"We're guilty of no deceit. You asked to be refueled and we complied. The hostages freed themselves, through their own resourcefulness and valor."

"You are right. They should be applauded, these brave civilians. I stand corrected."

Bennett and Dean exchanged uneasy glances.

"And now I have some news for you, something stimulating for your next press conference. I now hold the President of the United States of America as my hostage. . . ."

Around the Situation Room, faces fell and gloom settled in like a cold front.

"I haven't had the pleasure of meeting him yet—one of my people is bringing him up from the baggage hold, where he's been cowering, and creeping out of the shadows to murder brave soldiers from behind. But you would call that 'resourcefulness and valor' . . . perhaps on this score, we should agree to disagree."

"What do you want?"

"Soon we shall enter the sovereign airspace of Kazakhstan. You will cease your military escort at the border. If you violate our airspace, I will execute a member of the First Family."

And the click of the terrorist breaking off the connection echoed through the room, like the cocking of a gun. A big one.

Bennett said, "Back those fighters off now, General."

General Greely nodded and went to the phone.

Walter Dean had strolled over, out of the Vice-President's earshot, to have a word with the portly attorney general, Andrew Ward, who sat at the conference-room table like Jabba the Hut in a three-piece suit.

"Andrew," Dean whispered, "can't a majority of the cabinet declare a presidential incapacity? Or was my Harvard prof lying to me?"

"Your professor served you well," Ward said, "and so does your memory."

"Would you sign a document declaring an incapacity right now?"

Ward glanced at the Vice-President, dwarfed by the looming illuminated wall map, then said to Dean, "It would put her in charge, not you, Walter."

"She's holding up pretty well. Besides, I think I can sway her, if need be."

"What need do you anticipate?"

"The need to override a commander in chief who's being held by bloodthirsty goddamn terrorists."

A tiny smile formed on the pudgy face. "Did they teach you that at Harvard, too, Walter?"

"No. That was some advance graduate training here at

the Washington, D.C., School of Industrial Arts, Hard Knocks, and Cold Reality. Would you sign?"

"Under these circumstances, yes."

"You mind getting up, and seeing who else would?"

Ward nodded, hauled his heavy frame out of the chair, and trundled from the room.

The lean terrorist with the dead eyes led Marshall, Major Caldwell, Gibbs, and Shepherd through the lower deck and up the galley stairs. The other Secret Service agent, whose name Marshall was ashamed he could not remember, had died in the explosion of the hatchway door blowing. Eye signals from the other hostages to Marshall indicated their willingness to attempt to overtake the man with the machine pistol, but Marshall gave them tiny, barely perceptible head shakes, not to try.

Marshall knew that his fellow survivors, and he was no different, were physically depleted, wasted from the superhuman efforts it had taken to live through that hellish hurricane on the parachute launch ramp.

Anyway, all it would take was one burst from that machine-gun pistol to kill all four of them, in seconds.

And then where would Grace and Alice be?

No, Marshall had decided to go along with the terrorist, to let him feel smug, even standing with hands in the air as the terrorist stopped to use an intercom phone to alert his leader about his good fortune.

By Marshall's count, there were only three terrorists left. He would wait. He would assess the situation, and learn the status of his family, and make his move when the time was right. . . .

Now, with the machine pistol at their backs, the four

hostages climbed the winding stairs to the upper deck, offering no resistance as they were prodded into the lair of the beast who had done this thing. They moved into the world of blinking lights and glowing monitors and high-tech gear that was the Mission Communications Center, where only the floor, with its scattering of glass shards from a single broken monitor and occasional bloodstains, indicated the violence this room had seen.

Grace and Alice were seated in swivel work chairs, along the wall, and they were not bound; they looked fairly normal, his little family as he pictured them, Grace in sweater and slacks, Alice in sweatshirt and jeans. Marshall felt tears well up, and he thanked his God for answering one prayer, at least, and letting him see his family again. . . .

They bolted from their chairs and into his arms, and Alice cried, "Daddy!", and he soothed her with, "Angel," and he gazed into his lovely wife's face, her beautiful eyes doing their best to hold back the tears, her smile as luminous as it was brave.

Then other hands were on him, not the loving hands of his family but the rough grip of that cold-eyed terrorist, who was snarling, "Family reunion is over, you son-of-a-bitch," hauling him away from his girls, who now hugged each other, watching as the terrorist roughly duct-taped Marshall's hands behind him.

Another terrorist was training his MP-5 on Caldwell, Gibbs, and Shepherd, who were lined up against one electronic wall as if about to be executed. Marshall had not seen this terrorist before, but he knew at once, from the man's imperial bearing, that this was the leader. The devil-bearded, almost boyish countenance might have seemed almost pleasant; but the eyes were alive with death.

"We have not been introduced," the terrorist leader said, turning the gun on Marshall now, while his comrade began binding Caldwell's hands behind him in duct-tape handcuffs.

"I don't know your name," Marshall said. "But I know who you are. The pages of history are filled with . . . patriots like you."

"Ivan Korshunov," the terrorist said, and with the hand not holding the weapon, made a little gesture that, with a bob of the head, constituted a sarcastic bow. "It's an honor to have the President of the United States on the deck of my personal aircraft. . . . I like to think of it as the 'Flying Kazakhstan Statehouse.'"

The other terrorist was duct-taping Gibbs's hands now.

Korshunov continued, "Actually, it's the *only* state-house Kazakhstan has, at present. You see, a vicious terrorist blew up our real statehouse. Isn't that terrible? Such an atrocity?"

And now Shepherd was getting his hands duct-taped behind him.

Marshall, stealing looks at his frightened family, who remained huddled as if standing coatless in the cold, said, "I understand your point of view."

"Do you? Do you really?" Korshunov moved close to Marshall; they could smell each other's sweat. But the terrorist's tone remained cool, even cordial. "You've been a busy president, haven't you? But isn't that some-what undignified for a head of state? Ambushing my men from the shadows, darting in and out of your rat hole? Murdering three of Kazakhstan's bravest freedom fighters?"

And Korshunov backhanded Marshall, a sudden, vicious blow that cut the inside of his mouth and whiplashed his neck. Then a hard fist flew into Marshall's stomach, doubling him over, and Korshunov, his face distorted with fury, pushed the President down on the floor, and yanked him to his knees, shoving the snout of the MP-5 against Marshall's temple.

Marshall smiled, just a little. "Are you sure you want to do that? I'm what you came for, remember?"

Korshunov's features settled in their boyish mask again, and his voice returned to that soothing, cordial tone; with the same hand he'd used to backhand the President, Korshunov stroked Marshall's face, in mock affection.

"Thank you, Mr. President. Your wise counsel is always appreciated. . . . I must never forget how honored we are, to have you in our think tank—James Marshall, the nimble, charming dignitary who has solved so many problems for the weak people of other, lesser lands. . . ."

And with his gun, Korshunov pointed at Grace and Alice, as they stood clutching each other.

"I'll kill *them,* instead," he said sweetly.

Still on his knees, Marshall cried, "No!"

Korshunov nodded, saying, "Again, your wisdom prevails. Why kill both of them at once? Why not save one for later? Thank you, Mr. President."

"Don't do this. Are you a father, Ivan?"

The deadly eyes seemed to twinkle. "Why, yes. And I'm honored that you would address me by my given name. But I would never be so disrespectful as to call you James, or Jim; you are much too important for such a familiarity."

"If you're a father . . ."

"I *am* a father. With a lovely daughter, like yours. My family is why I make the sacrifices I do; for them, and for my country."

Korshunov began to strut, thinking.

He continued: "But you raise an interesting dilemma. What is a father, with duties to his family and to his country, to do? Here's a kindness I will pay you. I will shoot one of your females, right now . . . just one. But I will allow you to choose which."

Korshunov grabbed Marshall and whipped him around, and confronted him with the sight of his trembling family.

"Go ahead—choose!" And Korshunov's cordial tone was gone; this was the guttural grating of a madman, a monster. "You're used to sitting in your White House, playing God. Which one lives?"

Marshall's eyes locked with those of his wife, and he said, "Grace, I love you."

She smiled, chin quivering, eyes wet but brave, so very brave.

"Jim, I love you."

And her expression told him: *Give* me *to them; save Alice.*

Marshall turned hooded eyes on his captor: "I won't give you the satisfaction, Ivan. You can kill me, and you can kill my family, but you can't turn me into your accomplice, or your lackey."

Korshunov shoved Marshall to the floor, and planted a boot on the President's face, grinding him into the carpet like a cigarette he was putting out.

"Choose, you bastard," Korshunov said, "or I'll kill them slowly. . . ."

"What a message you're sending the world!" Marshall said, rage blotting out pain. But pressed down on the carpet, his hands were brushing something—a glass shard! "Is this what you came all this way for? Revenge against a man through his wife and child?"

The pressure from the boot let up. Marshall swallowed, breathed in hard, and slipped the glass shard into the palm of his bound right hand.

"You are right, as always, Mr. President," Korshunov said, the reasonable tone back, and he hauled Marshall to his feet.

"What do you want?" Marshall asked.

Behind his back, Marshall's bound hands worked the glass shard against the duct tape, trying to slice through the thick bands looping his wrists.

"What do you think?" Korshunov replied. "The release of General Radek. The world leader you kidnapped, who you abducted from his bed before blowing up his house of state."

"I can't do that," he said.

Marshall could only work at the duct-tape bonds slowly and easily; if he put much energy into it, the effort would show. . . .

"Then you die." Korshunov shrugged. "All three of you."

"Ask me for something I can give you. I would grant you anything to save my family. Safe passage. Amnesty. A fair hearing for your grievances. Even a trial for Radek outside Russia, in some neutral court—"

"Radek's release. Nothing else, nothing more."

"President Petrov would never allow that."

Korshunov's eyes and nostrils flared. "Please! Don't insult my intelligence. You are the most powerful man on earth! Now, suddenly, there are things you cannot do?"

And Korshunov smashed the butt of the machine pistol into Marshall's shoulder, sending a sharp stabbing pain throughout his whole upper body . . .

. . . but he didn't loosen his grip on the glass shard, and it didn't fumble from his captive fingers!

Then Korshunov pulled the stunned President over to a wall of monitors and shoved him up against it, hard knobs and switches and dials digging little grooves in Marshall's back, as if he'd been shoved against a thornbush.

"Stop with your fucking lies!" Korshunov raved.

"I tell you, Petrov won't listen to me."

Korshunov got right in Marshall's face. "Petrov is your dog, your pet dog. Ask him to bark on his hind legs and he is only too eager to comply. Tell him to *do* this!"

"You're mistaken about this, Korshunov. . . . Petrov manipulated me. My goal was to stop the bloodshed, but Petrov was after a personal victory. Petrov hates Radek."

Korshunov pushed Marshall against the wall again, then stepped away, strutting again. "Of course he hates Radek! The general is everything the Russian president is not: strong, brilliant, a man of vision, of true greatness."

"Petrov won't do it."

He was slicing at the stubborn bonds again, trying like hell not to give any outward indication. . . .

"You're saying he would refuse you? He would not help you save your family?"

"You haven't thought this through, Ivan—you're playing into Petrov's hands. You'd make him a hero, the leader who stood up to the terrorists and, even better, who stood up to the President of the United States."

Korshunov's eyes were flickering; he was considering Marshall's line of bullshit, despite himself. "You talk as though you had nothing to do with this."

"About what, Ivan?"

Was it giving? Could he use pressure from his wrists to tear loose, now?

Korshunov lurched over and shoved Marshall's face into a control panel . . . and the glass shard slipped from his grasp, dropping unseen to the floor.

"You engineered the kidnapping!" the terrorist stormed. "The destruction of our statehouse! And worse, your Western ways have infected our land, with that sickness you drape in the romantic meaningless word 'freedom,' but freedom without meaning, without purpose, is chaos, is degeneracy. You've handed my country over to gangsters and prostitutes! The same emptiness at the soul of your people eats now at mine."

"You're mistaken."

The slice from the glass shard had started a rip in the thickly wrapped tape; working his wrists, he could expand that rip . . . but his effort must not show . . . .

Korshunov snorted a laugh. "How do you think I got on this plane? I did it the American way, Mr. President. I paid off one of your people. This traitor of yours loves freedom, too, Mr. President. The freedom money, a lot of money, will bring . . ."

And Korshunov spat in the face of the President of the United States.

"Now," the terrorist leader said, hauling a telephone

from a counter over to Marshall, "make the call. No more diplomacy. No more negotiating. No more polite conversation . . . make the call."

"No."

Korshunov placed the phone on the floor and moved nimbly to Grace and Alice, and yanked the daughter away from her mother's protective grasp.

"No!" Grace blurted.

Korshunov brushed the dark blond hair away from the girl's temple and placed the nose of the machine pistol against the flesh, hard enough to pucker it. Alice began to whimper. To weep.

"Call Petrov," Korshunov said.

He wanted to rip those bonds apart, but they weren't giving way, they weren't giving way. . . .

He said, "Leave my daughter alone."

Korshunov's expression was a burlesque of sorrow. "To lose a child would be a terrible thing. They say it leaves you feeling so very . . . hollowed out."

"We're soldiers, Ivan, you and I. Take my life. Have you no honor?"

The tape was giving . . . but not enough . . . not enough. . . .

"If I kill you, could your wife or daughter tell Petrov to release the general, and get anywhere? I don't think so. I'll count to five. Remember when I counted to ten, before? Just to five, this time . . ."

"Daddy . . ." Alice whimpered, her face slippery with tears.

"One," Korshunov said.

"It'll be all right, honey."

"Two."

"Leave her alone!" Marshall cried.

"Three," Korshunov said.

"I'll do it," Marshall said. "I'll do it. Just leave my family alone."

And Korshunov stepped away from the girl, who flew to her mother's arms, the terrorist leader smiling smugly at the man who had been the President of the United States a few moments before, and now was just another hostage.

*Chapter Seventeen*____

In the middle of the Moscow night, in his expansive bookcase-walled office in a building complex that had formerly housed the Central Committee of the Communist party, President Stolicha Petrov had gathered many of his top advisers.

At a long oak table, they sat muttering among themselves, arguing, speculating, while the president, greedily smoking a cigarette, paced before the smaller oak table that served as his desk, with its array of telephones, one of which began to ring.

A male aide plucked the receiver from the phone, listened, eyes widening, then called out gently to his pacing president: "Sir . . ."

"Yes?"

The aide held the receiver out as if it were something that frightened him; perhaps it did.

He said, "The President of the United States . . . He wishes to speak to you."

With a world-weary sigh, President Petrov took the phone, eyes fixed on the view out the vast windows near his desk, looking onto the courtyard, where a pale moon washed the extra security staff patrolling out there in shades of ivory.

He listened to his ally's request.

"How can I say no to you, my friend?" Petrov asked. "If we must do this thing, we must. . . ."

And soon the phone was back on its hook, and the president of Russia was dismissing his advisers with an impatient hand. As they mutteringly removed themselves from his office, Petrov settled himself behind his desk and reached for one of the phones, to make a call that sickened him.

In the Situation Room at the White House, the Vice-President stood before the wall map tracing AFO's flight, bathed in its red-yellow-and-greenish glow. The secretary of defense, who had stepped from the room a few minutes before, was returning to approach her, a document held in both his hands.

But before Dean could speak, Communications Officer Peters called out to report an intercepted call.

"The President called Petrov," Peters said, rather numbly. "He asked him to release General Radek."

Walter Dean scowled, shook his head. "He can't do that."

"He must have no choice," Bennett said, sinking down into the chair at the head of the conference table.

"*We* have a choice," Dean said, standing beside her, leaning in on one hand, flat on the table. "Madame Vice-President, I have the signatures of a majority of the Cabinet attesting to the President's incapacity."

Dean placed the document before her, and she blinked at it, like a startled bird.

"Sign it," Dean said, "and the authority of the presidency will be yours."

She looked up coolly at him. "I could overrule Jim Marshall."

He nodded, smiling faintly. "Yes. And you need to."

"I can't do that. I won't do that."

Exasperation rushed out of him in a burst of wind. "Kathryn, the United States does not negotiate with terrorists! It's been a bedrock principle of this nation for twenty-five years. Give in to this, you declare open season on the United States. You open the door on countless American deaths."

"I know the risks."

He threw his hands in the air. "The risks? Kathryn, it isn't the President of the United States making this wrong decision, it's a husband and father trying to protect the lives of his wife and daughter."

"Can you blame him?"

"No." His expression was cold, not cruel. "But we can blame ourselves if we back that wrong decision, out of misplaced sentiment. History will judge you, Madame Vice-President, by what you do right now." He thumped a finger at the bottom of the document. "For God's sake, sign it!"

She smiled. "I admire your passion, Walter, almost as much as I admire your mind. Isn't it funny? *You* working so hard to make *me* acting president. . . . No, Walter, I won't sign this document. I stand behind my president."

His face turned ashen. "Thus goes a great nation."

"So be it," she said.

Within walking distance of the Bolshoi Theater, all but next door to Moscow's largest children's store, sprawled the Center, the former KGB headquarters that included the notorious Lubyanka Prison. The massive, austere, yellow-brick building, standing cold in moonlight, kept watch from its corner on the northeast side of Lubyanka Ploschad, a bustling square days and evenings, sleeping now.

In his private but hardly lavish cell within the concrete corridors of Lubyanka, General Ivan Stravanovitch Radek was not asleep. He had napped throughout the night, but he lay atop his cot, atop the blankets, in his full prison uniform, drab though it was, his shoes on, too.

He had begun this night knowing he had reason to believe this would be his last at Lubyanka Prison.

Alerted by the echoing of footsteps down the corridor, he rose from his cot and moved slowly into the meager moonlight fingering in from high barred windows. He stood almost at attention, waiting for the guards to reach his cell.

When they did, one of them—a young man whose pro-Kazakhstan sympathies were well known to the general—did his best to hide his pleasure in reporting, "General! Follow us, please. You are to be released."

And very soon, in a video security area of the prison, where a bank of monitors reported the general's progress as he marched through the prison, the Lubyanka security chief—not a pro-Radek man—distastefully handed a phone to a young soldier wearing the traditional Soviet uniform adopted by the Kazakhstan military.

"Hello?" the soldier said. "Yes. Yes, they're releasing the general!"

Radek was indeed parading grandly down the prison halls, the two guards more like an honor guard than an inmate escort. Other prisoners began to bang on their cell bars in rhythm, with cups and other metal objects, making a racket that rose to deafening proportions as the general's march of triumph continued. Some of the prisoners began to sing "The Internationale," the anthem of the Communist party, a rousing if not terribly harmonious rendition with counterpoint provided by the catcalls and boos of the nonpolitical prisoners among Lubyanka's population.

"No, no," the soldier said, swelling with pride, working his voice above the anthem that rang through the prison walls, "I will not hang up. . . ."

And on the other end of that phone, on Air Force One in Mission Communications Control, Korshunov was hitting a switch to pipe the spirited if off-pitch singing into the upper deck so that he and his men could also swell with pride.

Over the staticky singing, Korshunov said, "It's confirmed. They're releasing the general!"

Marshall said, "Okay, now what?"

"Now," Korshunov said, chin up, standing tall, swathed in the dissonant chorus of Russian political prisoners, "we return to our homeland, where General Radek will decide how best to make use of you."

"You said you'd release us," Grace Marshall said.

"Eventually, perhaps, we will," Korshunov said. "But now that we know that you . . . and your people . . . are willing to negotiate, well . . . Our small nation is in need of so many things."

A young male voice, above the off-key anthem, spoke in Russian on the phone line; Marshall knew enough of the language to get the gist: General Radek was going through some sort of processing station now, receiving his uniform and possessions.

Marshall caught Major Caldwell's attention; gradually, Shepherd and Gibbs brought their gaze to the President as well. He narrowed his eyes, trying to send them a message, trying to let them know that something was coming. . . .

Because Marshall was working at the rip in his bonds, and he was close to freeing himself; if the terrorist's attention was off him, long enough, he might be able to tear loose in one last wrenching of his wrists, Samson snapping his shackles.

Korshunov called out, "Kolchak! Andrei, put the Flying Shit House on autopilot, and join us in victory!"

A dark, sturdily built terrorist exited the cockpit through the blown-out entryway, grinning, drinking in the staticky sound of the Communist anthem as sung by the Lubyanka Prison Choir.

Korshunov embraced Kolchak, kissing him on both cheeks, and Kolchak returned the gesture.

Then, with a gratified sigh and a flower-child smile, Korshunov called to the lean, dead-eyed terrorist who was keeping an MP-5 trained on the hostages.

"Lenski! Sergei, my comrade . . ."

And as Sergei let his guard down to bask in the music and smiles and macho kisses bouncing around the room, Marshall snapped his bonds, reached out, and grabbed onto Korshunov by the gun hand, and when he wasn't able to wrench the gun free, put all his strength into shoving the fucking lead terrorist back over a table, then spun toward Lenski, who was bringing the MP-5 around to shoot at Marshall.

But Marshall grabbed onto the gun, still clasped in Lenski's hands, and shifted its snout—just as Lenski pulled the trigger—toward Kolchak, who took three of the spray of rounds from Lenski's weapon in the face, and slammed back into a wall of electronics, though the inside of his head had beaten him there.

Marshall slammed a forearm into Lenski's throat and the Russian went down choking, the MP-5 in Marshall's hands now, but when Marshall whipped around, Korshunov had grabbed Grace, and was using her as a human shield around which he fired three rounds from his machine pistol, two of them missing Marshall and destroying monitors, and the third would have taken the President down, but Shepherd, helpless on the sidelines with the other two duct-tape-cuffed hostages, leaped in the bullet's path, taking in his right shoulder the round that would have killed Marshall.

Grace shoved Korshunov away from her, and gave Marshall an opportunity to send a burst of MP-5 slugs in the Russian's direction. Korshunov, near the doorway, fell backward, struck in the vest, not wounded, just knocked down, and he was tumbling back, but reached out and grabbed Grace by the arm and yanked her down with him, out the door, down the stairs.

MP-5 in hand, Marshall was diving for the doorway when Caldwell called out, "Jim!"

And the President whirled and saw Lenski with his hands on the late Kolchak's weapon.

Marshall shot him in the head, a single well-placed round, not quite between the eyes, but close enough.

For government work.

"Daddy!"

His daughter ran to his arms, and he kissed her forehead, said, "Don't worry, baby, your mother will be fine." Nodding toward Caldwell, Gibbs, and the fallen, wounded Shepherd, he added, "Get their hands untied, would you, angel? Daddy doesn't have time. . . ."

And he was clattering down the stairs, machine pistol in hand, a wife to save, and a terrorist to kill.

*Chapter Eighteen*_____

At his oak desk in the spacious office in the former headquarters of the Central Committee of the Communist party, President Stolicha Petrov was partaking of a time-honored Russian custom.

He was slamming down vodka.

At the conference table, not imbibing, several of his top military staff, Generals Federof and Zinyakin among them, sat glumly listening, as did Petrov, to a musical presentation that sickened them.

On Petrov's desk, a line was open on a speaker-phone connected with the office of the security chief at Lubyanka; over this, unfortunately, they were being sub-jected to an off-pitch prisoner-chorale rendition of "The Internationale." A little drunk, Petrov regarded a small version of the Russian flag on a tiny stand on his desk.

With one finger, he flicked it off.

"All we've worked for," he said, more to himself than to his generals, "lost in one stupid moment."

Over the singing prisoners, the security chief's voice on the speakerphone said, "Mr. President, the Kazakh-stan helicopter is arriving."

"Position them outside the gate."

Then upon his generals Petrov turned a gaze made no less steady by the vodka.

"Place all forces on full alert," he growled, and emptied his glass.

Machine pistol in hand, Marshall corkscrewed down the winding stairs from the upper deck, three steps at a time, shoes clanging on metal, like warning bells resounding, joining the dissonance of the piped-in prisoner songfest of the Communist party anthem, which Korshunov's flip of the PA switch had apparently sent blaring throughout the plane, to every deck.

His sharp glance showed no sign of them down the corridor, but under the stairs, that carpeted floor panel had been thrown aside, leaving open the hatchway down into that ill lit world of the lower deck, whose every nook and cranny he'd made his own.

Looking down, all he could see was the feet of the dead terrorist in the galley; he yelled, "Grace! Grace!" and his voice echoed hollowly back at him.

But Grace's voice echoed back as well, from deeper within the lower deck: "Jim! Jim!"

He slid down the winding stairs as if they were a banister, and leaped over the dead Russian and through the galley, when a burst of MP-5 gunfire sent him ducking back, but not before he'd gotten a glimpse of Korshunov, Grace his human shield, backing down the gangway, apparently heading toward the tail cone, where the blown-open hatchway to the launching-ramp compartment and its rack of spare parachutes awaited.

Marshall dove from the kitchen and somersaulted

behind a strut, machine-gun pistol fire spitting at him while his wife screamed, "No, Jim, no!"

That staticky singing was getting broadcast to the lower deck, too, providing grotesque background music.

"Let her go, and I won't stop you!" Marshall called. "You can get the hell off my ship with my goddamn blessing!"

Korshunov, dragging Grace, called back, "Not until Radek is safely away!"

And the piped-in sound of that phone call would keep the terrorist informed, too. Right now, the voice of that young soldier, speaking in Russian over the singing, was saying, *"Comrades, our forces have arrived for the general!"*

"You hear that, Mr. President?" Korshunov screamed with maniacal glee. "It's almost over!"

"Jim, go back!" Grace pleaded, as her captor hauled her toward the tail cone. "Don't give up Radek! Call the Russians! Stop them!"

Korshunov reached around and smacked the woman on the side of the face, a close, open-handed slap that rang in the metal chamber.

Marshall's eyes narrowed, his upper lip curled back over his teeth, a wolf expressing displeasure. Staying low, not daring to return fire for fear of hitting his wife, he dashed down the gangway, bullets zinging above and around him, rounds careening off metal, before he ducked behind another strut.

But Korshunov was moving deeper and deeper toward the aft of the plane; Marshall couldn't make much progress, scrambling out on the gangway a few feet, bullets flying over his head sending him to dart behind a strut. The terrorist would be at the tail cone of the plane in moments!

"Double-cross me," Korshunov said, his near-hysterical voice echoing from deep down the gangway, the prison chorus accompanying him, "and your wife dies! Anything bad happens to General Radek, she fucking dies!"

Then Korshunov was lugging the First Lady through the twisted metal entryway where the door to the parachute launch-ramp compartment had been, and as Marshall made his way to them, he heard a hydraulic whine followed by the roar of gale-force wind, as within that compartment the lever had been thrown, the ramp lowering.

Marshall edged his way to the compartment entry, peeked in: Korshunov, his black hair seeming to stand on end in the rush of wind, like snakes rising from Medusa's scalp, already had his parachute on, keeping Grace covered with the MP-5 as she hugged the curved wall nearby, her hair, her clothing, whipping in the two-hundred-knot gust.

The noise, the deafening noise, was like being trapped inside a burning house as fire raged all around. At least that damn Communist anthem was drowned out, now. Peeking around the corner, wondering if he could get a shot off without endangering Grace, the President saw Korshunov, a terrorist to the end, hurling spare parachutes into the moonlit night, like an officer on the deck of a sinking ship tossing life preservers to overboard passengers, only Korshunov, of course, was achieving the opposite result.

Korshunov, tossing another parachute, glanced back in

Marshall's direction, to see if he was still coming, and Marshall reared back, not seen by the terrorist; then he peeked again as Korshunov cast yet another parachute into the night, and, hoping the churning wind would cover him, Marshall slipped into the compartment, ducking over into a gutter, where he at least he would have some cover if Korshunov spotted him.

Korshunov didn't.

Grace did, but showed nothing, as her husband edged along the wall, getting closer, moving around to where he could get a shot at the bastard that wouldn't put Grace in harm's way. . . .

And then Korshunov saw him, and pulled Grace to him, again making her his shield, and his eyes were wild, his hair dancing like snakes, as he screamed over the rushing wind, "Drop the gun! Drop the gun! Or I'll push her out now!"

Marshall, clothes flapping, knelt and placed the machine pistol on the floor.

"You don't need her now, Korshunov," he said. "You've won. Have some dignity!"

Both men had to scream to be heard, and their conversation had an hysteria that matched their wind-distorted faces.

"I'll be glad to leave her behind, Mr. President. You may need a stewardess . . . or perhaps a copilot!"

"Let her go! Then go ahead and jump! And good riddance!"

Head popping from around Grace's anguished countenance, Korshunov scowled. "You shouldn't have killed Andrei, Mr. President . . . put yourself in a bad spot when you killed my pilot! Who is there to fly the plane?"

And he shoved Grace aside and bent down and picked up a parachute by its strap.

"You see, Mr. President," Korshunov gloated, "this is the last parachute. . . . You're right: you lose, I win."

And as he began to toss out the last parachute, Grace charged him, pushed him backward, and the terrorist went stumbling off balance, instinctively clutching onto that parachute. As Grace withdrew from the sucking wind of the yawning tailgate ramp, to pick up the machine pistol Marshall had set down, the President was already in midair, leaping toward Korshunov like a lion turning on its trainer.

Then Marshall was on the bastard, the inferno of wind whipping both of them as they entwined like lovers, rolling, struggling, clawing, battling for the MP-5 still locked in Korshunov's right-hand grasp as they teetered at the edge of the launch ramp, where it took its steep decline into nowhere. Marshall got both his hands on Korshunov's gun hand and slammed the bastard's knuckles into the steel floor, and slammed them again, and again, until the sound of small bones breaking made a subtle, brittle accompaniment to the heavy-handed symphony the rushing wind was playing, and finally the Russian's fingers popped open and the gun went sliding down the ramp and dropping like a tiny stone into the bottomless ocean of the night sky.

With a howl of rage, Korshunov rallied, throwing a fist into Marshall, then another and another, climbing on top of him, while Grace looked on in helpless frustration— the MP-5 in her hands—only now it was she who could do nothing without endangering her husband.

Marshall flung the Russian off him, back deeper into the

compartment, away from the yawning ramp and the sucking wind, but Korshunov—his gun lost to the night—had hold of that spare parachute, and holding it by a strap, used it to bludgeon Marshall as he approached.

Marshall held up under the hammering blows, and relentlessly closed in, diving for Korshunov, taking him down onto the compartment floor, grabbing onto the parachute and looping the strap around the Russian's neck, wrapping that strap around his neck in a choking fashion.

But Korshunov managed to roll around on top, trying to pry Marshall's hand off that parachute strap. Grace, hovering nearby with the MP-5, still didn't have a clean shot!

Then Marshall's fingers found the rip cord on the spare parachute, and he knew exactly what to do.

"Time for you to deplane, asshole," he said into the terrorist's face.

And he yanked the rip cord.

The small deployment chute flew out of the pack toward the sucking opening of the ramp, where the wind caught it and pulled the main chute out into the sky, its sound like the fluttering of enormous wings.

"You heard me," Marshall said into the wide eyes of Ivan Korshunov. "Get the hell off my plane."

And the cord snapped taut, yanking Korshunov back at two hundred miles an hour, his neck twisted in the straps as it dragged him into the sky, snapping his neck, or to be more precise, snapping many bones in his neck and skull.

Grace flew to her husband's arms and they had one look out into the moon-washed night, where—before the

President of the United States hit the lever to raise the parachute ramp—they saw the would-be freedom fighter, one parachute on his back, unused, another whose strap was wound around his neck, and neither of them had done him any good, really: he was just a slack broken corpse under an ironic blossom of white, a footnote in history tethered to the end of a parachute, hanging limp, a flag that couldn't find a breeze.

General Ivan Stravanovitch Radek, standing tall and proud in his full-dress uniform, waited with regal patience as the guard opened the door onto the exercise yard. Never before had cement in the moonlight looked so magnificent; it seemed to Radek to glow with the promise of a new future.

The world had been taught, this night, that Radek was a force to be reckoned with; no minor player, but a major actor on the world stage.

As he stepped out onto the empty exercise yard, unaccompanied, the gate opposite him began slowly to open, and just beyond the gate, in the square, sitting proudly, was a helicopter with the insignia of his home. And around that helicopter, awaiting him, half a dozen soldiers in Soviet Kazakhstan uniform, who upon seeing him, snapped to attention and saluted. He grinned at them, stopped, and returned the salute.

What a glorious sight! He had dreamed of this moment, seeing his people, his soldiers, standing proud in the heart of Moscow, the city that had sold its soul to the West, the city that he would live to see regain its position as the capital of a rebuilt Soviet Union.

He walked slowly toward them, savoring the moment, his pride conspiring against him.

Marshall and his wife, arm in arm, hobbled down the gangway, hugging, kissing, lost in their reunion, when over the singing of the prisoners—still piped into the lower deck of Air Force One—came the voice of the young Russian soldier.

In Russian, he said, *"They are opening the main gate!"*

This sound froze both the President and the First Lady, bringing them back to a reality that, though Korshunov was dead, was still adversely, posthumously affected by the terrorist's evil maneuvers.

Grace's eyes were saucers. "What did he say?"

"He said they're opening the main gates."

She clutched her husband's arm. "Jim—you've got to get to President Petrov. Go! Go on without me. . . ."

Reluctantly but instantly, Marshall dashed away from his wife, up the gangway, through the galley, bounding over the Russian terrorist corpse there, scaling the stairs and finding his way to Mission Communications Control, where Major Caldwell was ahead of him.

"Korshunov's dead," Marshall said. "The plane is ours."

"Never had a doubt, Mr. President," Caldwell said, and handed him the phone. "I have an open line to President Petrov."

General Radek was halfway across the moonlit exercise yard, his eyes filled with tears at the sight of his brave men, when the siren began to wail.

Radek knew what the alarm meant: it signaled an escape attempt!

Suddenly the subtle lighting of the moon was blotted blindingly out as spotlights flooded the exercise yard. From bullhorns, guards shouted, in Russian, "Halt! Halt!"

And, incredibly, the gate before him began to slide shut!

Haloed in light, Radek, fit as any man under his command, broke into a run; he could beat it! He knew he could beat it!

His soldiers, as startled by this turn of events as the general, called out to him, encouraging him, and as guards charged into the exercise yard firing weapons, the soldiers fired back, laying down cover. Gunfire from high above the exercise yard joined in, and a small war broke out between the half-dozen Kazakhstan soldiers and seemingly countless guards, as Radek made for the helicopter, his feet on the first step when the bullet in his back dropped him dead to the concrete, just outside the prison gate.

In the Situation Room at the White House, Vice-President Kathryn Bennett, Secretary of Defense Walter Dean, Deputy Security Adviser Tom Lee, Generals Northwood and Greely, and all the rest, top advisers and lowly clerical grunts alike, had been listening to the depressing off-tune Communist anthem and the Kazakhstan soldier's play-by-play of Radek's release. Communications Officer Peters had tapped into the open line on Air Force One, and heads were hanging, faces cupped in hands of leaned elbows on the conference-room table.

But now the tone of the excited youthful voice of the Kazakhstan soldier had shifted from joy to dismay, as in

Russian he cried, *"The general is dead! They killed him! Do you hear me? Killed him! Oh God, oh my God . . ."*

Dean knew enough Russian to translate: "Christ, Petrov's had Radek shot!"

And the room fell silent, stunned, aghast with the thought of what this meant for the President and the First Family at the hands of the terrorists on Air Force One. The singing had stopped, but the young Kazakhstan soldier's sobbing continued, until Peters cut the sound at Bennett's wave of a hand.

"The world will hear only of an escape attempt from Lubyanka Prison," Dean said somberly.

Bennett's expression was curious, not cold, though there was a chill in her words: "Are you pleased, Walter?"

"Kathryn," Dean said, his face stony, his voice steady. "Jim Marshall is my friend. Alice is my godchild. . . . This is the worst moment of my life."

"Madame Vice-President!" Peters called, elated at his console. "I have the President on the line! They've retaken Air Force One."

Another stunned silence followed, but only momentarily, as cheers erupted, as Kathryn Bennett clasped Walter Dean's hand, tight, and the two adversaries traded tearful smiles.

On AFO, in the Mission Communications Center, Marshall was embracing his daughter, stroking her hair.

"Daddy, I was never so scared in my life," Alice said.

"Me neither, angel," he said, grinning at her.

"That awful man said you were a coward, that you ran out on us. . . ."

"He was wrong, wasn't he?"

She nodded and clutched her dad, and he patted her back, gazing at Grace standing nearby, who beamed at him with more love than any man could hope for in a lifetime.

"Girls . . ." he said.

"You're betraying your Republican roots," Grace said.

He tried again: "Ladies . . ."

"Not much better, Daddy."

"Women?"

Grace and Alice laughed and nodded.

But around them was the aftermath of violence: shattered monitors, blood-drenched carpet, a pair of dead terrorists, and a wounded chief of staff whom a Secret Service agent and an army major were tending.

Gently, Marshall said, "There's still work to be done. Why don't you go down to our stateroom and do your best to relax?"

After quick hugs and kisses, mother and daughter trotted down the circular stairs to the main deck.

Marshall knelt over the unconscious Lloyd Shepherd as Gibbs dressed the chief of staff's shoulder wound and Major Caldwell looked on.

"How's he doing?" Marshall asked the Secret Service agent.

"Not good," Gibbs said. "Normally, this wouldn't be a fatal wound, but he's losing a lot of blood. We gotta get this crate on the ground."

Marshall looked from the face of one man to the other. "I don't suppose either of you would happen to know how to fly. . . ."

"No, sir," Caldwell said, Gibbs not bothering to answer, busy with Shepherd's dressing.

"Well, keep me company anyway, Major," Marshall said, heading toward the blown-open entryway that led to the flight deck. "I'm going to get on the horn and see if I can't wrangle a long-distance copilot. . . ."

Chapter
Nineteen____

Slicing through gray, moon-pierced low-lying clouds, Air Force One—for all its bulk, graceful as a glider—was the picture of man's mastery of nature, via machine.

From the outside.

Within, wearing a bloody, torn shirt, a battered, exhausted fifty-year-old man who had not flown any type of aircraft in twenty-five years was settled into the pilot's chair, headset on, looking above him at the overhead panel, thinking it looked like the inside of a TV set, lightly, tentatively fingering switches, muttering, "Hydraulic power . . . engine ignition . . . alternative gear selection . . . lighting . . ."

In the copilot's seat beside him, Major Caldwell glanced from the wide double windows and their view of a vast empty moonlit night to the President of the United States, who was now gazing with tight eyes at the control panel before him, with its dials, push buttons, switches, knobs, levers, gauges with seemingly hundreds of quivering needles, and readout-littered computer screens, all casting a greenish glow that gave the impromptu pilots an airsick look.

"Sir," the major (also wearing a headset) ventured too casually, "what kind of aircraft have you flown?"

Right now, autopilot was flying the plane and doing a damn fine job of it; the President's hands had yet to settle on the two horns of the wheel.

"Oh," Marshall said, and he grinned over at Caldwell with a youthful embarrassment that might have been endearing under other circumstances, "helicopters, mostly . . . This is my first jet."

Caldwell tasted his tongue, then formed a smile to reassure Marshall of his confidence, but it was a sickly smile, exacerbated by the control-panel glow.

"Well, hell," Caldwell said, "I've always been a big believer in on-the-job training."

In their headsets, the two men heard a familiar voice: "Mr. President, Major Caldwell, this is Colonel Jackson."

Marshall smiled over at Caldwell, who returned the smile, nothing sickly about either grin now. Bob Jackson was Air Force One's backup pilot and both men had flown this ship with him, many times.

"Hey, Bob," Marshall said, the quaver in his voice barely perceptible. "How'd that Notre Dame game come out? I kinda got called away from the tape of the damn thing."

"Then I'm not gonna spoil it for you, sir," Jackson said. "You can watch it on the ground."

"There's a plan."

"Sir, we need to get you out of hostile territory."

"Not a bad idea, Bob."

"I want you to look just above your central video screen."

"Central video screen," Marshall muttered, and his eyes found the monitor and he said, "Got it."

"There's a series of red LED numbers. One of them should read one-one-zero."

Marshall's eyes found them. "Got 'em."

"That's your heading. Below that readout, look for a knob surrounded by hash marks. See it?"

"See it."

"Turn that knob counterclockwise until your course reads two niner-zero, repeat, two-niner-zero."

Marshall followed instructions and, still on autopilot, the big plane began to turn.

"At two-nine-zero," Marshall said. "This big baby's correcting herself."

"Super," Jackson said. "That will get you the hell out of Kazakhstan."

"Which is exactly where I want to be."

"Roger that. Now, you can't land the plane on autopilot, so let's go over a few things."

Marshall swallowed. "Why don't we?"

Just behind him, Grace and Alice were coming up into the cockpit.

"Just a moment, Bob," Marshall said. "Get lonely?"

"Alice wanted to be with you," Grace said. "Me, too."

He didn't really want them here; if something went wrong, he'd rather they didn't see it coming out the huge cockpit windows. He didn't say this, but his expression must have conveyed it, because Grace responded to his concerns.

"We need to be together," she said, "whatever happens."

Marshall nodded, and said to Grace, "Why don't you

take the flight engineer's seat, and Alice, there's an observer's seat behind me, that folds down. . . ."

"I see it, Daddy."

"Now, I'm going to be on the horn, here," he said, pointing to his headset, "getting us on the ground . . . so do your cheerleading silently, okay, girls?"

They smirkily smiled at his use of "girls" and he gave them a goofy, mock-innocent look, saying, "Hey, I was spellin' 'girl' with no 'i' and lots of 'r's'. . . . Doesn't that make it okay?"

Alice shook her head, still smirking, but fondly, very fondly. "Daddy," she said, "that's so two years ago. . . ."

"Well here's something fresh off the news wire," he said quietly, voice barely audible above the thrum of the 747 engines. "I love you both."

And he turned back to the control panel, saying into his headset, "Let's get started, Bob. I guess you're never too old to learn. . . ."

In the Situation Room at the White House, the pilot who'd been chosen to talk the President down sat at the long conference table with a group that included Vice-President Bennett, Defense Secretary Dean, Deputy Security Adviser Lee, and the two generals, Northwood and Greely. All eyes were on the thirty-five-year-old, tanned, fit, brown-haired pilot, dragged from home in the middle of supper, told to come as you are, in civvies (a sportshirt and slacks), hunkered over the phone with an intense expression not betrayed by his nonchalant voice.

"Now, Mr. President, I want you to find your airspeed and altitude."

"Shouldn't they be little dials, right in front of me?"

"They're not dials anymore, sir. They're on the video screen just in front of the yoke."

"Okay."

Bennett was looking back at the wall map. "Where's the nearest safe landing site?" she asked Greely.

"Insirlik, Turkey," the general said.

Suddenly, on the huge glowing map, a small cluster of icons popped on, and immediately started inching forward toward the larger icon that was Air Force One.

Bennett said to General Northwood, "What the hell is that?"

But it was Greely who answered: "MiGs, Madame Vice-President," then under his breath, "Goddamnit, MiGs . . ."

"My God," Northwood breathed. "They're on a course to intercept Air Force One."

"Christ!" Dean was on his feet and moving toward the map, looking up with the expression of a farmer spotting a flying saucer in his field. "They took off from Aktyubinsk. The commander of that base is a Radek loyalist. . . ."

Northwood exploded. "But Jesus Christ, Radek's fucking dead! Beg your pardon, Madame Vice-President."

"No problem, General," she said. "You're right. He is dead, but we may have a fucking martyr on our hands. . . . Well, let's make our position known on the subject. General Greely, order our fighters into Kazakhstan. Authorize them to use any and all means to protect our president. . . . Any problem with that, Walter?"

He was smiling tightly at her. "None whatsoever, Madame Vice-President."

*   *   *

In the cockpit of his F-15, Major Frank Carlton felt adrenaline surge through him. He gave an order in his headset and the five jet fighters under his command dropped back into formation with him.

Halo Flight Squadron was about to get back in the game.

From the bottom of Carlton's plane, the fuel tank under the fuselage detached, plummeting to earth; then a burst of flames shot from the tail of the F-15 as it accelerated past the speed of sound, the other F-15s following suit, afterburners blazing, racehorses out of the gate, tails on fire.

And in the cockpit of Air Force One, James Marshall was in the middle of a flying lesson.

Colonel Bob Jackson's voice was in Marshall's headset: "When you're on final approach, keep the throttles about mid-range."

"Understood."

Then there was another voice in Marshall's headset, a familiar voice: Kathryn Bennett's.

"Mr. President, we're tracking six MiGs closing on your position."

"Oh, shit."

"I've sent our F-15s to protect you."

"God bless you, Kathryn."

And Kathryn was off the phone.

Major Caldwell, who had also heard the Vice-President's news over his headset, looked at Marshall numbly and said, "MiGs?"

Marshall raised an eyebrow, a little, not wanting to alarm his wife and daughter. "That's what she said. I don't think she's in the mood for practical jokes. . . ." He turned toward Grace and Alice. "Better strap in; the captain would turn on the seat-belt sign, if he knew where the hell it was. We might have some turbulence coming up."

Buckling in, Grace asked, "What's a MiG?"

"High-speed, high-altitude jet fighters," Alice said, ever the student of CNN. "Of Soviet design."

"Just like the good old days," Caldwell said. "General Radek would be proud."

"Bob," Marshall said into the headset, "if those MiGs show up before the F-15s can stop 'em, I'm gonna need to maneuver this big bird. How do I turn off the autopilot?"

In his headset Marshall again heard Jackson's voice: "Just push the button on the yoke; it's by your left hand."

"Just like cruise control . . ."

"That's right, sir. Just like cruise control."

Marshall thumbed the button on the left horn of the wheel. Caldwell winced as the autopilot disengaged, but no jolt followed, the ride remaining smooth, as if nothing had happened.

"Got it," Marshall said. "So far so good. I'm gonna make a left turn . . . no hand signal. . . ."

"Make your movements smooth and slow," Jackson's voice in the headset advised, "till you get the hang of it."

"No prob, Bob," Marshall said, and Caldwell was smiling, really smiling; smooth sailing. "Gonna try a right now. Step on the ball . . ."

"Yes, sir," Jackson said. "Comes back to you, doesn't it? Like riding a bike."

"These MiGs . . . How close are they?"

"I'll get back to you in a second on that," Jackson said.

Then a sudden loud buzz made everyone on the flight deck jump, as if jolted by a mild electric shock; and a computer display came boldly alive with the words: RADAR LOCK.

"Never mind, Bob," Marshall said into the headset. "Company's here."

And they were, racing up in tight formation behind Air Force One, which seemed to lumber in comparison to the sleek MiGs, which then fanned out in the moon-streaked sky as their leader drew a bead on the jumbo jet, a missile flaming from underneath the MiG's wing, thrusting toward the President's plane.

In the cockpit of AFO, Caldwell pointed redundantly to the red blinking light on the control panel, pulsing like a blush of embarrassment on the impromptu pilots' faces.

"We got one coming at us," Caldwell said.

An LED display popped on: ACTIVATING COUNTERMEASURES.

Marshall was easing the plane to the left, while a computer read-out said: LAUNCHING FLARES.

Flares rocketed from either side of Air Force One, the MiG's missile veering as it neared the plane, turning tail to trail the heat of the nearest flare, plunging toward the ground, to cause its damage far below, somewhere in the countryside. On AFO, they didn't hear the explosion as a Kazakhstanian barn exploded.

Marshall, hands tight on the yoke, had overcompensated somewhat, and the plane was rocking side to side; but they hadn't been hit. They were safe.

"Jesus, that was a squeaker!" Caldwell said.

"Daddy, are you all right?"

"Fine, angel," he said, but muttered, "We need the damn cavalry, and soon. . . ."

Caldwell spoke into his headset. "U.S. Fighters, this is Air Force One," he said, "we are under fire, repeat, we are under fire. Where the hell are you?"

"Air Force One," a voice came into the headsets. "This is Colonel Carlton, Halo flight leader. We are closing on your position, repeat, closing on your position."

"ETA?" Marshall asked.

"Two minutes," the F-15 pilot replied.

"We may not be here in two minutes, Colonel."

"Hang tough, sir. We'll nail their asses to the sky, when we get there."

As if in defiant response to Colonel Carlton's confidence, a Bronx cheer of cannon fire erupted in the night, tearing bullet holes in AFO's right wing.

"We're hit!" Caldwell yelled.

"Thanks for pointing that out," Marshall said tightly, yoke bucking.

The MiG responsible swooped past the cockpit window in further defiance, jerking into a vertical, even as fuel began to leak from the damaged wing. Soon flames were dancing in the darkness, orange and red and yellow: the outer engine was on fire.

"We've got an engine on fire," Marshall said into the headset. "Number-four engine is on fire!"

More red warning lights had clicked on, deepening the red pulse on the flight deck. Grace and Alice Marshall sat draped in fear, taking the white-knuckle flight to end all white-knuckle flights; but they did not weep, and they did not scream or give in to hysteria or in any way hinder what the man in their family was trying to do for them.

"Sir, pull the fire handle overhead!" Jackson said, speaking from a Situation Room where eyes were glued to the moving icons on a luminous electric map with the action like a grotesque football game, Air Force One trying to make it to the end zone that was the Kazakhstan border.

"I've got it," Caldwell said, pulling the bright red fire handle above him, discharging extinguishing halon gas into the number-four engine.

"Jesus," Marshall said, jerking at the wheel, "we're rolling right!"

The engine whirred to a halt as the gas suffocated the fire, and it felt good to look out and see those flames gone; but now Marshall had only three engines, and the controls were off-whack!

"Left rudder!" came Jackson's voice in the headset. "Left rudder, sir—you've got to compensate!"

Like a driver braking at a deer, Marshall stomped down with his left foot, and the plane straightened out. "Should I ease off on the number-one engine?"

"No," Jackson's voice told him. "It'll slow you down. You'll have to trim it out."

"How do I do that, exactly?"

"Knob. Aft pedestal."

Some new red warning lights had blinked on, and Caldwell gestured to them with a finger, as if he were trying to brush them away. "This doesn't look good, Jim. . . ."

Marshall glanced where the major was pointing, then into the headset told Jackson, "We've got some new lights on. We're turning into a goddamn Christmas tree."

"What do they indicate?"

"They indicate we're losing fuel."

Another MiG swooped in, or was it the same one? Tracer fire smacked against the plane, thudding like one rock after another being hurled at them.

"We got a MiG strafing us," Marshall yelled into his headset. "They can't hurt us with that stuff, can they? We're bulletproof, right?"

"Roger that," Jackson's voice said reassuringly.

But in the cockpit of AFO, his copilot's next words were less reassuring.

"Shit!" Caldwell yelped, "we've lost countermeasures!"

Marshall's eyes landed on the flashing computer readout: SYSTEM FAILURE.

Grace Marshall reached over and clasped her daughter's hands. They smiled at each other, their chins quivering; they had no tears left.

Colonel Carlton and his men were closing fast, the F-15s flying in the Wall of Eagles formation as they came upon the MiGs, swarming like hornets around the big sluggish bird that was Air Force One.

In his cockpit, Carlton was issuing an order: "Halo Flight—everybody lock a bandit."

But the MiGs were still outside "max range" on Carlton's control-panel computer display.

"Halo Flight Leader to AFO," Carlton said, "almost in range, Mr. President!"

"We've got full system failure," the President's voice said edgily. "We have no countermeasures. It's time for you to get busy, Colonel."

Carlton's eyes were on the computer screen, his fingers on the trigger.

Then, speaking to his own men, Carlton said, "Halo Flight—stand by for max range! And . . . Fox Three!"

Carlton fired; so did his men, six AMRAAM missiles igniting as if one from one rapid-fire weapon, streaking from the F-15s, and the MiG that had been riding AFO's tail met the first of the missiles and exploded in a ball of flame.

The MiG pilots hadn't seen the Americans coming—in fact, "Americans!" was the last word spoken by the pilot of the second MiG to meet a missile and explode into fiery nothingness.

But now they did, six F-15s emerging from the darkness like angry bats out of hell—and bringing hell with them.

"Splash two," Colonel Carlton reported, "splash two . . . Four more bandits bearing zero-nine-zero. Halo Flight, engage."

And the F-15s peeled off to pursue the quartet of remaining MiGs.

"Air Force One," Carlton said, summoning his president, "bug out west at ten thousand feet. We'll cover you."

"With pleasure," the President's voice came back.

Carlton watched as Air Force One took a steep angle down—the commander in chief was handling that barge pretty well!—pulling away from the pack of MiGs, who were breaking away as Carlton's men closed in.

But one of the MiGs looped around to follow its monstrous target.

"Sir, pull up!" Carlton yelled into his headset. "You got one on your tail!"

"Well, get him *off* my tail," the President ordered.

And in his headset, Carlton heard Captain Chris Kafer saying, "I'm on it. Halo Two is Tally one. I'm engaged."

In the cockpit of AFO, that old, familiar, irritating buzz emanated from the control panel, accompanying a computer display: RADAR LOCK . . . COUNTERMEASURES UNAVAILABLE.

"They got us in their sights, Major," Marshall said. "Christ, we're sitting ducks."

"This is Halo Two, sir," a new voice in his headset said. Another sound was mixed with the voice: static and an electronic tone, then static and an electronic tone. Marshall didn't realize this indicated the pilot's computer trying to lock the MiG on target; the pilot explained: "I'm on him but can't get a lock . . . hang steady."

But a Kazakhstan pilot, in the cockpit of his MiG, had a tone from his computer so clear, so pure, it was like a victim's high-pitched scream: perfectly locked onto his target—Air Force One—he fired.

Captain Kafer, coming up fast in his F-15, saw the speeding missile breaking straight for AFO, and yelled into his headset, "Sir, missile away! Break left, break left!"

On AFO, Marshall pushed the plane into a hard turn, but his computer wasn't impressed: SYSTEM FAILURE, it said, MISSILE LOCKED, it taunted.

Where was the readout that said, KISS YOUR ASS GOOD-BYE? Marshall wondered.

"We're too slow," Caldwell said, not afraid, resigned to it. "He's got us."

Marshall turned to Grace and smiled. "I love you, darling," he said, and she nodded, and he looked at his daughter and said, "You're the best, angel," and she said, "I love you, Daddy," and Caldwell said, "Jesus H. Christ!"

All eyes in the cockpit went to the window and the whites of those eyes showed all around as they took in the sight of an F-15 screaming out of the darkness and right at them, right at the window.

Then it was gone, ducking under the nose of the plane.

"What the hell . . ." Marshall said.

They could not see the act that would win Captain Christopher Kafer his posthumous Medal of Honor. They did not see him, in his F-15, zoom into the path of that missile, like a Secret Service agent stepping in front of an assassin's bullet for his president.

The thunderous explosion sent fragments of the fighter plane battering against AFO like nasty hailstones, rocking it badly, shrapnel ripping away a good portion of the tail section.

"Two's down," Colonel Carlton's voice called out in Marshall's headset, "two's down! Air Force One, are you with us?"

Marshall, manfully steadying the plane, said, "We're still here. . . . Thanks to a brave soldier."

And the President of United States, grateful yet again for the life of his family, wiped wetness away from his eyes with the back of a grease-smudged fist.

Out the cockpit windows, the triumphant MiG pilot was paying his contemptuous last respects with a gloating canopy roll, zooming into the sky.

In his headset, Marshall heard Colonel Carlton's response to the MiG's victory dance: "Not so fast, you son-of-a-bitch!"

Marshall did not hear, of course, the Russian pilot's

cry, in his own language, to his fellow pilots: "He's on me! I need help!"

But Marshall did see Carlton's F-15 coming up behind the MiG, sending a missile screaming toward it, and before the Russian pilot could reach his ejection lever, the fighter plane exploded into flames and fragments.

"A little payback, Mr. President," Carlton said, but Marshall wasn't one to gloat over the death of any soldier, relieved as he might be to see this one go.

He was equally relieved to see those other three MiGs hightailing it into the night, disappearing through moon-misted clouds, and then it was as if this ivory-kissed sky had never been filled with fighter planes, cannon blasts, rocket fire, and burning death.

And the President could hear, in his headset, as one of Carlton's pilots reported in: "Halo One, this is Halo Three. Our three remaining MiGs are buggin' out. We're clear."

For all the relief in the cockpit of Air Force One— Grace and Alice unbuckling themselves to embrace, the President and Major Caldwell slapping a high five— there was as much anxiety. Emergency lights were flashing like some psychedelic disco; fuel gauges read low, autopilot was out, their systems well and truly fried.

"Get back in your seats, girls," Marshall said, and with no objections of political incorrectness, his wife and daughter strapped back in. Into his headset, Marshall said, "Bob, you still with us?"

Jackson's voice, from the White House Situation Room, came over Marshall's headset loud and clear: "Right here, sir."

"We still got problems. My rudder's not right. Sluggish as hell."

"Could be hydraulics."

Now Colonel Carlton's voice, from his F-15 flying nearby escort, came over the headset: "I'll drop back and take a look."

A few moments later, Carlton's voice returned: "Man, your tail's all shot up, leaking fluid. Torn up pretty bad, sir. You got any elevator control?"

"Not much. Sluggish as hell, too."

"Guess you know what this means, sir."

"I believe I do."

Now Marshall realized Colonel Carlton's F-15 was flying right alongside him; he could make eye contact with the pilot.

Who was saying, "Sorry, sir."

"Thank you for your help, Colonel. You and your brave men."

"Listen, I'll stay on your wing. Take her out straight and steady, till we figure somethin' out. We didn't come this far not to beat this thing, did we, sir?"

"You got that right, Colonel."

"Sir, you did yourself proud today. Your country, too."

And Carlton snapped his commander in chief a salute, and his commander in chief crisply returned it.

Then an awful silence descended on the flight deck of Air Force One.

On the map at the White House Situation Room, the icons representing Air Force One and the F-15s moved across the Kazakhstan border into friendly Russia.

Kathryn Bennett sank into her chair with a relieved

sigh. Just down the conference table, Colonel Bob Jackson was still maintaining phone contact with the President, working out whatever bugs needed working out. All that was left, really, was for Jackson to talk Jim Marshall down, and after all, Marshall was a pilot; it would be touch-and-go, with a big plane like that, but these two were up to it.

Colonel Carlton's voice, beaming from the cockpit of his F-15 over the speakers in the Situation Room, wiped the relief off Kathryn Bennett's face, and the other assembled faces.

"Okay," Carlton said, as nonchalant as if reporting the weather, "we got a little problem here. Sirs, Madame Vice-President—Air Force One is badly hit. With the damage, there's just no way in hell they can land."

*Chapter Twenty*_____

In the Situation Room at the White House, the Vice-President and the secretary of defense were pacing in opposite directions before the looming electric maps, like loved ones in an emergency-room waiting area who expected bad news. But the two generals were planted at parade rest before the maps, military statues guarding the gates of government, eyes searching those glowing maps, each man shuffling through mental computer files.

"They can't control the plane," Dean said, his tone cheerless, "their engines are failing and they're losing fuel."

"They're alive on that ship, right now," Bennett said as the two passed in their pacing. "This is no time to give up."

"Kathryn, even a crash landing is impossible. They're going to crash, and they're going to die." He stopped pacing and looked right at her; she stopped, too. "We should call the chief justice in."

To be available to swear her in as president.

She turned to her generals. "Isn't there anything we can do for them? There must be *something* we can do!"

Pointing to an icon on the map that traced AFO's precarious path, Greely said to Northwood, conversationally, "Is this your airstrip strike team?"

"Yes it is. Why?"

Eyes still on the map, Greely smiled to himself, shook his head, as if considering an idea that might be crazy or brilliant or both. Then he turned to his army counterpart and said, "Bill, just how good are those Rangers of yours with those Herc transports?"

"Sam, they could teach your boys a few maneuvers."

Greely's eyes tightened but also twinkled; he put a hand on Northwood's shoulder and said, "Then let's give them the opportunity to prove you right."

Twenty-three minutes later, prepped for his part in an air rescue of a sort that had never before been attempted, James Marshall—still at the wheel of the lumbering Air Force One, guiding the beast as best he could with what few controls were still responding—said, "If anybody has to use the latrine, I would say now's the time."

His daughter, behind him in the folded-down passenger seat, said, "I'm fine, Daddy. Dad?"

"Yes, angel?"

"Are we still on for Camp David?"

"Oh, yeah. Big time."

"Good. 'Cause everything's gonna be okay. This is gonna work."

"I know it is, angel."

Grace said, "Well, I don't know about the 'latrine,' but I can use a potty break," and unbuckled herself and went out as her daughter and husband chuckled.

Major Caldwell, in the copilot's chair, said, "I had all my precious bodily fluids scared out of me a long time ago, on this trip."

"You've been great, Norm. Couldn't have made it through without you."

"You know, I always knew you were a good president," Caldwell said. "Now I know you're a hell of a guy. Pleasure serving at your side, sir."

And the two soldiers shook hands.

"What's their ETA?" Caldwell asked.

"About two minutes."

"Good. That's about how much fuel we got left."

Marshall turned toward Mission Communications Control. "Gibbs! Come up here a second!"

Caldwell said, "Those Hercs are designed to haul paratroops, not do midair rescue."

"They're also refueling barges," Marshall said. "I think this is a good plan."

"Well, yes, so do I," Caldwell said, but he didn't sound any too sure, really.

The Secret Service agent came up into the flight deck and dropped into Grace's empty flight-engineer seat. "Shep's conscious."

"That's a relief."

"Don't get your hopes up too high, Mr. President. He's stable, but he needs a doctor."

"There'll be one on the transport."

A rosy blush at the base of the sky hinted at dawn's arrival.

In Marshall's headset came a new voice: "Air Force One, this is Liberty Two-Four. Do you read?"

"Loud and clear, Liberty Two-Four." Marshall turned back to Gibbs. "Get that door open."

The Secret Service agent nodded curtly, and as he

was leaving, Grace Marshall was coming back up, taking the seat.

Out the cockpit windows, twinkling like extra stars in a morning sky still draped in night, came the approaching navigational lights of the Lockheed C-130H transport.

Marshall said to his wife, "They're here, honey. We're going home."

They exchanged tiny loving smiles, and Marshall returned his attention to the wheel, telling Caldwell, "We gotta slow down a little. Gimme flaps five."

On the main deck, Gibbs was crossing to the forward cabin door, where he read and followed the directions on the door for its emergency release. A lever disengaged the door with a vacuum pop like a gigantic can of coffee had been opened, the rushing air flapping the Secret Service agent's clothing as the emergency slide raft deployed and inflated, then ripped loose and wafted away in the two-hundred-knot wind, a bright yellow cloud disappearing into the predawn sky.

Gibbs could see, hanging on to a wall strap, looking out the open door braving the rush of air, the bulky, camouflage-coated, prop-driven C-130 with its high-riding wings making its tortoiselike approach, its rear ramp door wide open.

In the AFO cockpit—Grace and Alice out of their seats and crowding around the pilot and copilot chairs—the view was astonishing. The C-130 was practically on top of Air Force One.

"Super flying," Marshall said breathlessly.

A helmeted Army Ranger was in the doorway of the open rear ramp, clipping onto the end of a wide thick cable, other Rangers gathered around him.

Then the Ranger stepped off.

Alice gasped, and Marshall felt his stomach muscles tighten like steel cords.

The Ranger had hopped out of the plane and into the sky, where, dangling like a worm on a fisherman's line, he was lowered by his fellow Rangers, winched down toward the big fish that was Air Force One.

Soon the Ranger was slapping against the side of the ship, which he plastered himself to, like a sky diver who changed his mind, sliding along the surface of the plane, dragging himself along the fuselage, until he got to the open cabin door, grabbing the edge, Gibbs hauling him inside.

Immediately, the Ranger—a young black soldier, his face blessed with the hard, strong angles of a warrior—hooked that three-inch-thick cable to a metal clasp near the top of the door frame.

"We're hooked!" the Ranger said into his headset, then looked to the man who'd helped him in.

"Secret Service," Gibbs identified himself, having to work to be heard over the rush of wind that fluttered his clothing, tie lifting from his neck like a rope on a noose.

"Where's the President?"

"On the flight deck. The cockpit!"

And in the cockpit, the voice in their headsets was telling Marshall and Caldwell, "AFO, Liberty Two-Four is hooked and ready to move into rescue position."

"Roger," Caldwell said, just as more red lights added to the festive array on the control panel, and an engine ground to a halt. "Liberty, we just lost another engine."

"Number two out," Marshall elaborated.

"Liberty Two-Four acknowledges," the voice in their

headsets said coolly. "Just try to hold her steady. Pretty soon we're not going to need any engines."

"That's good," Marshall said, "'cause pretty soon we're not going to have any."

A rustling behind him caught Marshall's attention, and he turned to see the young Ranger coming up into the cockpit.

"Welcome aboard Air Force One, son," Marshall said.

A white smile blossomed in the black face. "An honor and privilege, Mr. President." Then the smile was gone, and he was all business. "Sir, it's time to go."

"Who's going to fly the plane?"

"I'll take over, sir. You and Major Caldwell and the ladies need to get down there."

As he rose to comply, Marshall caught one last incredible view out the cockpit window: in the predawn sky, the darkness starting to fade, as if it were wearing out, the C-130 Herc (the sight of which took him back to Vietnam) was in a lateral position to AFO, connected to it by a hundred yards of cable, down which an Army Ranger was sliding.

"Let's go," he told his family, and he and they and Major Caldwell crawled out of the cockpit, whisking through Mission Communications Control with its dead bodies and shot-up high-tech gear and a groggy Lloyd Shepherd, down the winding stairs to the sucking wind of the open cabin door, where the second Army Ranger—having just sailed into the plane—was unclipping from the cable.

The Ranger—another kid, this one rosy-cheeked if steely-eyed—turned to salute the President and say, "Sir! We have orders to take you off at once, sir."

Marshall stood between the women of his family, an arm around each. "My family first."

As they spoke, another Ranger in snatch harness made the slide from the C-130 onto Air Force One, unclipping as he hit the open doorway, stumbling, recovering quickly. Then another followed the same process.

"Sir," the second Ranger said. "I have my orders."

"Now you have new ones, from your commander in chief. My family first!"

"Yes, sir!" And into his headset the Ranger barked: "Move into position! Ready to convoy First Daughter at commander in chief's direct order."

And outside that open cabin window, they could see the big noisy transport craft hovering, then dropping, dipping down with that cable following, until the C-130 was to the side of and below Air Force One, a hundred yards of cable linking the two planes, like a thin line drawn in the sky.

The Ranger got behind Alice and, with Major Caldwell's help, harnessed the girl to him, and hooked her harness to a traveler strap, then told her, and her father, "We're set, sir."

"Daddy!"

"Alice," he said, "it's gonna be okay."

"Promise?"

"Yeah. And that's not a campaign promise."

The child's mother, who was getting harnessed to her own Ranger, yelled over the wind and prop noise, "You can do it, darling! Just hold on tight!"

The girl took a deep breath as the Ranger shoved off with his precious package held tight to him, sliding from the lip of the doorway down the wire, sailing through the blasting wind, plummeting the hundred yards to the waiting door at the rear of the C-130, where Rangers grabbed onto them, guiding them into the transport.

The rosy-cheeked Ranger, listening at his headset, said to the President, "Liberty Two-Four has the First Daughter safely aboard, sir."

Caldwell grinned and slammed a triumphant fist into an open palm as Marshall beamed at Grace and she beamed back at him. Then the smile dissolved as her Ranger moved her into position, clipping himself on, then her, saying, "We're ready, ma'am. Sir."

Suddenly she was trembling; or was that just the churning two-hundred-knot wind? "Jim . . ."

He was getting into another of the harnesses the Rangers had brought with them; Gibbs and Caldwell were doing the same.

"I'll be right behind you, baby," he told her.

And the Ranger, hugging the First Lady, stepped into nowhere, sliding away from Air Force One, gliding down that wire with surprising ease and grace, to be pulled aboard the C-130.

"Liberty Two-Four reports the First Lady safely aboard, sir," the rosy-cheeked Ranger said.

"Yes," Marshall said softly.

"Come on, sir!"

"Norm, wait here," Marshall said to Caldwell, and looked at Gibbs. "Let's haul Shepherd down."

Gibbs nodded, and the two men started toward the winding stairway to the upper deck.

"Sir!" the Ranger called. "You're next!"

"No I'm not," he said, from the stairway. "We have a wounded man to transport."

Then the President and the Secret Service agent who had seen them through so much of this calamity lifted the wounded chief of staff and carried him down the stairs.

Shepherd was groggy, but managed, "No, Mr. President. You need to go. You go."

"Shut up, Shep," the President said.

"Won't you listen to me, for once?"

"No. Don't worry about me, Shep."

But in the AFO cockpit, the first Ranger aboard, who was in the process of rigging straps to the yoke as a makeshift autopilot, was staring into a control panel where yet another red warning light was flashing.

Into his headset, the Ranger said, "We've lost number-three engine!"

Which left one engine.

In his headset, the Ranger heard the Herc pilot saying, "You're losing altitude too fast. We can't get back into position to send another team over. You have to get the President out of there, now!"

As if to prove the C-130 pilot's point, the 747 dropped into a rapid descent.

The wounded Shepherd, clasped to his rosy-cheeked Ranger chaperon, had already made the halfway point on the downward slide toward the transport's waiting open rear door when this sudden altitude drop brought the C-130 up higher than Air Force One, and the two men began to slide back.

Marshall, observing this from the doorway, felt his stomach sink, and Caldwell gripped the President's arm, tight.

But then the C-130 compensated, dipping down, doing a damn good job of maintaining a position beneath AFO as it lost altitude, and Shepherd in the grasp of the Ranger made the rest of the journey to the arms of the Rangers in the Herc doorway.

"Incredible flying," Caldwell yelled, shaking a victorious fist in the air.

The black Ranger came bounding down those winding stairs from the upper deck, boots clanging on metal, calling out a report to Marshall, Caldwell, and Gibbs, "Liberty Two-Four reports casualty safely aboard!"

"All right," Marshall said, "Major Caldwell, it's your turn."

"Stop it, Jim. You've got to get off this plane!"

The Ranger said, "Sirs! Just a moment!" He was listening in his helmet's headset. His stony expression betrayed a little something. "Liberty Two-Four says we're passing six thousand feet. Impact in less than two minutes . . ." The Ranger looked pointedly to the President. "Sir, get ready. We've got to go now."

Marshall said, "Can't you get another team of Rangers on here, so we can get these men out?"

The young Ranger's expression was grave as he snapped the metal ring of a traveler strap on the line, for him to clip his harness onto. "No time for the other team, sir. I can only take one more."

"No," Marshall said. He'd come too far to lose these men! "We're all going."

"Sir, that's impossible. I have to take you."

Caldwell stepped forward, unbuckling his harness and letting it drop to the floor; though he still had to work to be heard above the din of wind and props, there was a quietness about Caldwell's voice—a grave dignity.

"Mr. President, you have a greater responsibility. You know that. It's time for you to leave the plane."

The Ranger stood poised at the doorway, about to clip onto the traveler strap, awaiting the final decision when it came from an unexpected source, a shot ringing out, then another, two rounds slamming into the young soldier, sending him back through the open doorway, a sky diver who forgot his parachute, but it didn't matter, because this brave young man was already dead.

Marshall, grabbing onto the traveler strap that the Ranger had never hooked onto, whirled, as did Caldwell, and they saw Gibbs, with a handgun he'd lifted earlier from the corpse of Kolchak, pointed toward them. Gibbs, harnessed up and ready to go, wore an expression as empty as his morality.

"You!" Caldwell said. "You were the fucking traitor!"

"No," Gibbs said quietly, the tiniest of smiles etching itself on thin lips. "You were, Major. At least when *I* tell the story. I was only protecting the President."

And the traitorous Secret Service agent shot Major Caldwell through the heart; he collapsed, dying in moments, as Marshall, the traveler in one hand, hanging on to it like a subway strap, looked down in shock and dismay at the sprawled form of his fallen friend.

"You bastard," Marshall said. "I trusted you with my life. . . ."

"So will the next president. Give me that strap."

"Come and take it—you're going to shoot me, and pin it on the major, right? Only, if I let go of *this* first . . ."

"Give me the fucking strap!"

They could both feel the huge jet plunging downward, like a comet burning to earth.

And Gibbs reached for the strap in Marshall's hand, but that still left the President with his right hand, which he used to whap Gibbs's gun hand, knocking the pistol to the floor, where it clunked out of reach. Gibbs managed to keep his balance, and dove at Marshall, but another right-hand presidential punch rocked Gibbs, only Gibbs was no pushover, he was, after all, a trained government agent and he came back for more, and Marshall gave it to him, smashing the fucker's features to a pulp as the pride of the Secret Service desperately struggled to clip onto that traveler strap.

The ship had no engine now; no one was there in the cockpit to see it, but the altimeter had plummeted, and the last of the engine lights flickered out, AFO diving into a banking twist, pulling the slide-for-life cable taut. The pilot of the transport could not keep up that kind of pace, not diving through two thousand feet. No way to compensate . . .

Marshall had maintained his balance, hanging on to that subway strap, but Gibbs got tossed like a drunk's lunch, and was on the floor now, his face a bloody mess, fingers and half-battered-shut eyes searching for that fallen handgun.

The President had the upper hand now, and could make his escape. Only, he couldn't. He looked out the cabin door in the gale-force wind and the lightening sky and saw that his rescue line had pivoted from a downward angle to an upward one. He clipped on, but what good would it do? You can't go sledding up a hill. . . .

Then Gibbs made a desperate lurch at Marshall, but the transport plane, unable to follow Air Force One in its nosedive, pulled sharply up, drawing the cable taut to where it broke its clasp over the cabin door and yanked the President out of Air Force One and into the sky.

If Gibbs screamed, Marshall couldn't hear it. His ears were filled with the sound of the big plane plummeting, and the prop-driven engines of the bulky Herc above him doing their best to pull up into a steep climb, taking him for a hell of a reverse bungee jump.

And below him, not so far below but getting farther as the C-130 pulled out, the Flying White House exploded in the Russian countryside, killing a traitor much too quickly, the fireball licking up after Marshall, but not reaching him.

He could hear the voice of a Ranger in the Herc above him: "Winch him up! Winch him up!"

Where he was clipped onto the end of the cable was precarious, the clasp caught where the hook had broken off, really just held there by some chunks of twisted metal, and he held on to the cable with his hands, flesh tearing, his grasp turning slick with blood, barely able to hold on, and he thought of Grace and he thought of Alice and he thought of the brave men who had died on this mission, some of them in the glowing wreckage below him, but not of the cowards, not of the terrorists, only the heroes, and the belly of the big clumsy C-130 got closer and closer. . . .

In the Situation Room at the White House, yet another terrifying radio show was playing over the speakers. Eyes rimmed with raccoon circles of exhaustion, Bennett and Dean and Lee and Northwood and Greely and Attorney General Ward and the rest sat at the conference table or at workstations around the room and listened to history writing itself down.

It would have some help from those in the Press Room, whom Bennett had allowed (over Dean's objection) to hear, along with them, the pumped-in air traffic between a civilian tower and the pilot in the Army Special Forces C-130 transport.

And finally the C-130 pilot spoke the words they had been dreading all day: *"Blue star, Air Force One is down. . . ."*

Bennett and Dean exchanged a solemn glance. Before her was the document that, with her signature, would have given her presidential power, not so long ago; now, she would not need it. Now, it would be time to call the chief justice. . . .

"I repeat, Air Force One is down."

Another voice replied: *"Liberty Two-Four, this is Tower. Do you have the President?"*

No response. Around the conference table, heads hung.

"Liberty Two-Four, do you have the President? Over."

"Stand by."

"Liberty Two-Four, this is Tower. Please report. Over."

"We read you loud and clear! Stand by!"

Vice-President Bennett covered her face with one hand; then she felt someone clasping her other hand. She looked up. It was Dean. His smile was tight and brave and reassuring.

"Liberty Two-Four announces change of call signs," came the voice of the C-130 pilot. *"Please alert all air traffic. Liberty Two-Four is now Air Force One. Repeat, Liberty Two-Four is now Air Force One. . . . President safe aboard."*

In the Press Room, the normally cynical crew cheered, while the Situation Room—a stationary vehicle that, in its way, had been held hostage even longer than Air Force One—erupted into hugs and tears, as relief and joy flooded the room.

And Kathryn Bennett, with a smile that transformed her haggard features into those of the beautiful woman who had entered this room hours before, ripped the document before her into several shreds, then stood to face the secretary of defense.

"Job well done," he told her.

"Job well done," she told him.

They shook hands, and she took her time leaving, shaking hands with her coworkers along the way, sharing congratulation and jubilation.

Attorney General Ward lumbered to his feet. "She might have been president."

"She may be yet," Dean said. "And here's a thought. . . . How would you like to be the Democrat, next time, who has to run against President Rambo?"

Ward savored that, and smiled, waddling from the room as Dean, bone tired as he was, not normally what you'd call a "people person," set about to shake every hand in the place.

On Air Force One—which is to say, a certain C-130 transport—the President of the United States, hauled unceremoniously aboard by a gaggle of Rangers, returned a salute to a fresh-faced young soldier who reminded him of somebody.

Himself.

"Welcome aboard, Mr. President."

"Good to be home, soldier," he said, and went to the waiting arms of his family.

The ungainly new Air Force One took its position at the center of its F-15 escort squadron and, this long terrible night finally over, headed into the sunrise. It hurt the eyes of all aboard, but that was to be expected. Tomorrow is always brighter, in America.

EATERS OF THE DEAD

In the year A.D. 922, Arab courtier Ahmad Ibn Fadlan accompanies a party of Vikings to the barbaric North. Ibn Fadlan is appalled by Viking customs—their wanton sexuality, their disregard for cleanliness, their cold-blooded human sacrifices. And then he learns the horrifying truth: he has been enlisted to combat a terror that slaughters the Vikings and devours their flesh.

CONGO

Deep in the heart of the Congo, near the legendary ruins of the Lost City of Zinj, a field expedition dies mysteriously and brutally. In Houston, Karen Ross watches a gruesome video transmission of that ill-fated team. In San Francisco, an extraordinary gorilla with a 620 "sign" vocabulary and a fondness for finger painting has drawn a replica of the frayed, brittle pages of a Portuguese print dating back to 1642, a drawing of the ancient lost city. Immediately, a new expedition is sent into the Congo, descending into a secret world where the only way out may be through the grisliest death.

SPHERE

In the middle of the South Pacific, a thousand feet below the surface of the water, a huge vessel is discovered resting on the ocean floor. A group of American scientists rushes to investigate, and what they find defies their imaginations: a spaceship of phenomenal dimensions, apparently undamaged by its fall from the sky. And, most startling, it appears to be at least three hundred years old.

JURASSIC PARK

An astonishing technique for recovering and cloning dinosaur DNA has been discovered. Now one of mankind's most thrilling fantasies has come true. Creatures extinct for eons roam Jurassic Park, and all the world can visit them—for a price.

Until something goes wrong.

RISING SUN

On the forty-fifth floor of the new American head-quarters of a Japanese conglomerate, a grand opening celebration is in full swing. On the forty-sixth floor, the dead body of a beautiful young woman is discovered. The investigation begins, and the Japanese saying "business is war" takes on a terrifying reality.

DISCLOSURE

An up-and-coming executive at the computer firm DigiCom, Tom Sanders is a man whose corporate future is certain. But after a closed-door meeting with his new boss—a woman who is his former lover and has been promoted to the position he expected—Sanders finds himself caught in a nightmarish web of deceit in which *he* is branded the villain. As he scrambles to defend himself, he uncovers an electronic trail into the company's secrets—and begins to grasp that a cynical and manipulative scheme has been devised to bring him down.

THE LOST WORLD

It is now six years since the secret disaster at Jurassic Park, six years since the extraordinary dream of science and imagination came to a crashing end—the dinosaurs destroyed, the park dismantled, the island indefinitely closed to the public.

There are rumors that something has survived.